MISCHIEF

in the

Morgue

A Sydney Hayes Mystery

Misty Lynn

ACKNOWLEDGMENTS

I'd like to dedicate this book to my IT computer wizard, Ryan Corwell. Without your unwavering dedication to troubleshooting my countless technical mishaps, this book may never have come to print. A heartfelt thank you goes out to my wonderful reading group—Deanne, Scott, Ryan, Darlene, Derek, and Tisha—for your endless support and patience as you tirelessly gathered to help me untangle the mistakes I often make. Each gathering is not only productive, but an occasion filled with laughter and fun. I also want to express my gratitude to my esteemed beta readers, Judy Baker, Deanne Cooper, and Heather Placek. Lastly, I would like to extend my appreciation to the courageous men and women of our armed forces for their remarkable service and sacrifices. Your dedication to our country inspires us all and allows us the freedom to pursue our dreams.

CHAPTER 1

It was a beautiful, sunny mid-June day. I heard the cheerful melodies of birds and enjoyed the invigorating scent of fresh air. I was looking forward to enjoying the day. The last couple of weeks since I returned to my hometown had been hectic, to say the least. Two murders would ruin anyone's week.

I crawled under the shower spray, relishing the warm water as it cascaded over my tired muscles. The knowledge that I was on leave from the Army for the next few months allowed me to relax momentarily. However, these thoughts were short-lived. They were shattered by the faint, ominous creak of my bedroom door slowly swinging open.

"Gina, you there?" I yelled.

No response came, which seemed weird since I left the bathroom door cracked open, so she should have been able to hear me.

"Gina!" I yelled again, feeling myself tense.

As I reached for the shower knob, I turned it off and stood still, straining to hear any sound. The silence was palpable. I let out a slow breath and gently rolled my neck to relieve the tension in my muscles. It was important to remind myself that I was not in the African jungle or trekking across the Sudan. I was not on a mission. Instead, I found myself in the small town of

Gettysburg, known to most for its war history. I knew it for being one of the most boring towns in America. Apart from the two murders last month, but that was a fluke.

As I reached for the shower knob to turn the water back on, a sudden thud echoed from the bedroom. It was the kind of sound made when someone collided with a dresser or bedpost. In that moment, I felt fortunate to have always possessed a sixth sense when it came to detecting danger. Just then, the hairs on the back of my neck stood on end, and a chilling sensation slithered down my spine.

I soundlessly pushed the shower curtain open and removed my gun from its perch on the back of the toilet. I focused my aim on the door, which was slightly ajar, and braced myself for the arrival of the intruder. There was no way I would let myself be caught off guard and possibly meet my end while I was in the shower. Especially when I was naked.

The door slowly crept open. I held my breath and waited. And then, in emerged a sleek, motorized robot. It was equipped with a camera perched atop its frame and a single arm extended from the center of the machine just below the camera. The robot moved gracefully on tracks, resembling a tank.

I swiftly snatched a towel from the rack and flung it over the machine. Then, I hastily grabbed another towel and wrapped it around myself. I stormed out of the bedroom and descended the stairs. I found Gina seated at the kitchen table, surrounded by scattered electrical components. Her laptop took center stage as she focused intently on the screen while holding a controller that resembled the kind used in video games to kill off zombies.

"What the hell?" I exclaimed.

She looked up from the screen, feigning innocence. "What?"

"Don't give me that. You sent a robot into my

bathroom. With a camera, no less!"

A mischievous grin spread across her face. "What do you think of Marti?"

"Marti?"

She nodded with excitement. "That's what I am calling him. It stands for Military Acquired Robotic Technology Investigator. Marti for short."

"Military acquired? Did you steal him when you left the Army?" I drop my head into my hand. "Please tell me you didn't steal an EOD robot?"

Gina was my aunt. She retired early from the Army last year due to medical reasons. She was an Explosive Ordinance Disposal specialist, essentially a member of the international bomb squad. These specialists used robots similar to the one that invaded my morning shower to safely deactivate bombs. I would estimate these robots cost around half a million dollars. The last thing I needed was for government agents to burst in and arrest us for stealing military property.

Gina gestured dismissively. "Anytime one of the robots malfunctioned or broke down, the Army would just scrap it. The government is incredibly wasteful like that," she said, shaking her head. "I salvaged some of the discarded items and parts when they threw them away. I rebuilt Marti to use him in my investigations. He can access locations I can't and can take pictures."

After returning to our hometown last year, Gina established her own private investigation business. She's been causing havoc on the town ever since.

She beamed joyfully as she exclaimed, "He still needs a few tweaks, but he is running great. Today was his first test run."

"Well, my shower is not a peep show, so keep him out of my bathroom."

I felt a gentle tap on the back of my leg and glanced down to see Marti's arm extended, rubbing my calf. "He made it back down here quick." I had to give props to the robot for its speed. The ones I had seen in the Army took forever to get from one place to another.

Marti circled around me and glided over to the table. Gina grabbed it and carefully set it down next to her laptop.

"I've made a lot of modifications. He's way faster and smaller than the original prototype." She picked up a screwdriver and began adjusting its arm. "I'm planning to install a small microphone so he can eavesdrop on conversations and some video technology. Then he'll be all set to start working."

I shook my head and returned up the stairs to finish my shower. My aunt Gina was an expert when it came to electronics and bombs, but she often lacked common sense which explained some of the predicaments she had gotten into over the years.

* * * *

Every morning began with a familiar routine: a plate of scrambled eggs, crispy strips of bacon, and a steaming mug of rich coffee, of course. My morning was incomplete without the invigorating jolt of caffeine, an essential ritual that propelled me out the door. After three weeks of staying with my aunt and having eggs and bacon every morning, I contemplated it being the only breakfast she knew how to make. I wouldn't complain out loud because the eggs were always perfectly scrambled, light, and fluffy, while the bacon's edges were crisped to perfection. Truthfully, my cooking skills were limited to barely boiling a pot of water, so who was I to critique her?

After breakfast, I stepped outside for a stroll through the neighborhood. The crisp morning air filled my lungs. Feeling a bit stiff, I paused to stretch, raising my arms high above my head, eager to loosen up. At that moment, a sharp pain pierced through my side, causing me to wince involuntarily. It was a stark reminder of the circumstances that had led me to live with my aunt, a weight I carried with me.

As I began my walk, I noticed Jean, the neighbor across the street, watering her array of pink and yellow flowers on her front porch. Jean, an elderly woman with silvery-gray hair, had it set in tight rollers that tugged her eyebrows skyward, giving her a startled expression as if she had just seen a ghost.

"Good morning, Jean," I yelled as I waved.

"Good morning, Sydney. Enjoy your walk," she replied, her voice warm and inviting, as the screen door creaked open behind her.

Suddenly, a shaky, hoarse voice echoed from inside the house, "Who are you talking to?" The words carried a hint of curiosity, punctuated by faint rustling as someone shifted within.

Jean lived with her ancient mother, Beatrix, who was likely a teenager when the Egyptians erected the pyramids. Beatrix shuffled onto the porch, her frail frame moving slowly. She released her grip on the screen door, which swung back with a loud bang.

"Who's that?" Beatrix hollered from the front porch, squinting through her Coke bottle glasses. Her vision was so bad she probably wouldn't even notice I was standing here if I didn't move.

"It's Sydney," Jean replied, her tone patient as she gestured towards me. "Remember, she is staying with her Aunt Gina, who lives across the street," Jean explained.

"Is she the one that stole Tom?" Beatrix raised her cane high and whirled it around her head. The movement was so unexpected that Jean ducked to avoid the potential whack.

I was told Beatrix's cat died a decade ago, a fact she couldn't seem to remember. I shook my head as I continued down the sidewalk.

"You better return my cat." Beatrix's voice trailed behind me.

I began my walk at a leisurely pace, feeling the stiffness in my muscles from weeks of inactivity. Each step reminded me of the ache in my chest, a lingering discomfort from my injuries. As a counterintelligence agent for the Army, injuries were an unfortunate part of the job, but this one had left its mark. Memories flooded back to that fateful night of my last mission, a hot and muggy evening thick with tension. It was an ideal setting to take down a notorious drug dealer.

But fate had other plans. From a nearby rooftop, an unseen assailant fired, and I found myself hit by two bullets that lodged in my chest. I was whisked away from Germany and airlifted back to the States for medical care. After nearly a month surrounded by sterile white walls and the beeping of machines in the hospital, I was finally discharged and sent home to recuperate.

Opting to stay with my aunt instead of my parents felt like the right choice. While my parents were well-meaning, my mother was a force to be reckoned with. She was eager to see me settled down, married, and producing grandchildren. I wouldn't have been surprised if she offered a dowry to attract eligible suitors. As I walked, I looked forward to regaining my strength, eager to be back at one hundred percent so I could return to my position with the Army and return to my apartment in Rome.

I circled the block twice until I felt out of breath, then I returned to the house. The bullets that punctured my lung and cracked a few of my ribs had left me with a long road to recovery, but I was confident that after several months of rest and reconditioning, I would be as good as new.

Just as I managed to push one foot through the front door, I was suddenly mowed down by a whirlwind of fur. With a thud, I found myself sprawled flat on my back on the cool porch, the breath momentarily knocked out of me. The furry brown ball sat on my chest and enthusiastically licked my cheek.

"Wilbur, down," Gina called out from inside the house, her voice cutting through the stillness of the afternoon. The animal gave my cheek one last lick with its rough, sandpaper-like tongue before leaping off my chest. It sat at Gina's feet.

I maintained my position sprawled out on the porch and contemplated the questionable sanity of my decision to stay with Gina. The thought of the local jail crossed my mind. It would be safer for me to stay there than in this unpredictable place.

"Are you alright?" Gina asked, her voice laced with concern as she stretched out her hand to help me up from the ground.

"Yea, just got the wind knocked out of me." Not to mention the pain that was shooting through my chest. I grabbed her hand, pulled myself up, then turned my attention to the woolly beast. Its eyes were hidden by a mountain of hair, but not enough hair that you couldn't see its tongue lolling out in a goofy display.

"What is that?"

"His name is Wilbur." Gina scratched him behind the ear, causing the creature to stomp his back leg on the floor like the rabbit from the animated film. "He belongs to my friend Dixie. Her sister down in Florida fell and broke her arm, so Dixie is going down there for a few days to help. I always watch Wilbur when she's out of town."

"And what will you do with him while you're at work?"

"He can either accompany me to the office or stay here. He is incredibly well-behaved. Come on Wilbur let's go outside."

The mobile mop followed Gina into the kitchen.

"Do you think letting Wilbur in the backyard with the flying demons is a good idea?"

When Gina purchased the house a year ago, she inherited the property and two feisty chickens that roamed freely in the backyard. They made their home in a rickety shed at the edge of the yard. To everyone else, they seemed to be nothing more than quirky companions, but they were a feathered nightmare to me. Every time I was in the yard, they would take to the air, flapping their wings like tiny, chaotic dragons, ready to swoop down and peck at my head. Because of them I exclusively used the front door to come and go.

I was worried the dog would attack the chickens, but the more I thought about it, it seemed like a good idea. I was looking forward to the chickens getting what was coming to them.

"I think he is more of a herding breed than an attack breed," Gina remarked.

She pushed the screen door open, and Wilbur burst forth like a cannonball. He sprinted eagerly towards the oak tree and sniffed around the base before peeing on it.

The moment he darted across the yard, the chickens caught sight of him, their beady eyes wide with surprise. They froze in place, rigid as statues. Wilbur continued his explorations. After a few more moments of sniffing around the grass, the dog zeroed in on the chickens. His gaze locked onto them with an intense curiosity.

Sad to say I held my breath with anticipation of the upcoming fight. The dog bounded happily towards the frozen chickens. He skidded to a halt just inches from Lacey and flopped down in the warm sun, panting. The chickens, noticing the intruder had stopped moving, tentatively waddled over to investigate. They circled him like two wary fighters sizing up a competitor, their heads bobbing with curiosity.

The dog simply smiled and panted as he observed their antics. After several laps around the dog, Lacey jumped up onto his back. The pecking of Wilbur's head I expected never happened. Instead, Lacey nestled down in his thick, plush fur. Not wanting to be left out, Cagney joined in and settled down beside Wilbur's face, her feathers brushing against his snout. Wilbur huffed in contempt and closed his eyes.

I exhaled sharply, frustration bubbling within me as I shook my head in disbelief. Unbelievable. With their feathery bodies and beady eyes, the chickens seemed to relish tormenting me every chance they could. Yet, here they were, inexplicably choosing to befriend their natural adversary. The irony of the situation left me at a loss for words.

Gina's phone rang, breaking through the room's silence and she walked out to answer it. I decided that after the morning I had I needed another cup of coffee or maybe the entire pot just to revive my spirits. I was happy that I was starting to get back into shape, but when the dog bowled me over, the pain in my chest was so sharp I had a flashback to the night I was shot. I was lying on the ground, bleeding, thinking I was taking my last breath. I shook my head vigorously, trying to dispel the haunting memory. I wondered how long the pain would last before it subsided completely. Would I have to live with it for weeks, months, or years? My train of thought was abruptly cut off as Gina stepped back into the room.

She brushed a strand of hair behind her ear and said, "Walter just called. He needs me to come by his office to discuss a case." Her brow furrowed slightly, revealing her sense of obligation. "I promised Dixie I would take Wilbur to his grooming appointment today, but now I'm caught in a bind. Would you take him for me?"

"I've never taken care of a dog before." Despite growing up in an old farmhouse, we never had a pet. The closest we came was the hamster my sister accidentally squeezed to death when she hugged it. We only owned the poor creature for a day. I don't hold it against her; after all, she was only four years old at the time. After college, I jumped straight into military life, which offered little room for pet ownership.

Gina waved her hand dismissively. "All you have to do is walk him to the groomer, then drop him off at the office when he's done," she explained, her tone light and encouraging. The thought seemed deceptively simple.

She pointed to the coffee table in the living room, where I could see his leash and collar resting. She instructed me to have him at the groomer by one o'clock before she headed out the door, leaving me with the prospect of a new experience that felt both daunting and alarming.

.

CHAPTER 2

I dedicated the morning to doing laundry and cleaning the kitchen. Every so often, I peered through the screen door, curious about the antics of the animals outside. I watched as they frolicked around the yard in what looked like a game of chase. Eventually they settled down in the cool shade of the old oak tree for a nap.

Since I didn't cook, I thought about going to the diner for lunch but quickly dismissed the idea knowing that dogs weren't welcome in such establishments. Instead, I resigned myself to making a simple peanut butter and jelly sandwich. As I took a bite of the dry, stale bread it struck me that I had yet to set foot in a grocery store since my arrival in town weeks ago. With the help of a glass of cold milk, I managed to get the sandwich down.

After placing my dishes in the sink with a soft clatter, I strolled over to the screen door. I whistled and called for Wilbur while opening the screen door. The ball of fur erupted towards me, much to the dismay of the chickens, who started clucking and hopping from one foot to the next as if angry. Wilbur bounded into the house and followed me into the living room, his tail wagging excitedly.

I picked up the leash and examined what I initially thought was a collar. It turned out to be a peculiar device. It was a forest green object shaped like a bone, adorned with dangling straps at each corner with plastic clips at the ends. Holding it up, I turned it over in my hands, angling it in different directions, trying to decipher how it fit on Wilbur. In a moment of determination, I draped it over Wilbur's back, eliciting a 'Don't be stupid' look from him. After five minutes and two YouTube videos, I felt I had it figured out.

As I went to place the harness on Wilbur's back he took off and trotted into the kitchen. I followed him and found him backing up against a corner.

"Wilbur, we have to put your harness on so you can go get a haircut."

He made a whining noise that I swear sounded like he said, "I won't."

I placed my hands on my hips, the leash dangling to my knee. "Come over here now," I ordered.

He backed up into the corner, obviously not convinced of my superiority. With his front paws on the ground and his butt up in the air he looked like a cat ready to pounce. A low, playful growl escaped him. I dove for him, but he nimbly sidestepped me and dashed back through the doorway. I blew out a breath in frustration. This was going to be a long afternoon.

After several more attempts and some successful bribing with leftover bacon, I finally wrestled him into the harness. After the leash was secured into place, which I managed to figure out on my own, there was only one chrome metal loop on the back of the harness, making it a no-brainer. With the harness now in place, Wilbur settled down, and we leisurely strolled down the sidewalk toward the groomers. It was a beautiful summer day.

Thousands of tourists flocked to Gettysburg

each year to immerse themselves in the rich history of the battlefields and the historic buildings that date back to the eighteen hundreds. The main streets were buzzing with people trying to catch a glimpse of the past while reenactors brought history to life with vivid detail. The street that Gina's house sat on was part of the historic district but was far enough off the beaten paths that the sidewalks were relatively quiet. The street became more crowded as we approached the town center, but Wilbur seemed unfazed. Instead, he ignored the people and stopped every few moments to sniff every fire hydrant and tree we passed.

As we arrived at the groomer, I was surprised to see that the name had changed. It had once been called "Stylish Pooch," but now a new sign hanging from the corner of the doorway proudly announced, "Stylish Pooch and People." The street billboard outside said, 'Live nude dogs. Free lap dances.'

The glass-fronted shop revealed a fresh coat of mint green paint inside. The room originally only had a few chairs in one corner. The previously sparse room now boasted a variety of furnishings, including a sleek beautician's chair with a chrome base and black leather padding. A woman I didn't recognize stood behind it, trimming a man's hair with stainless steel scissors. Next to her was a sink with a reclined black leather chair designed for shampoos.

On the opposite side of the room, a plum-purple leather chair with a detached footrest waited for clients. Next to it, a lilac-colored table displayed an assortment of colorful nail polishes, files, clippers, and various tools that could be used for medieval torture. A young woman in her early twenties, with one side of her head shaved and the other flaunting vibrant hot pink hair, sat on a round, backless stool, casually filing her nails.

Genesis emerged through the doorway leading

to the back of the shop. On a previous visit, I found out that this was where the dog grooming happened.

"Sydney, what an unexpected surprise," Genesis said as she hobbled over to me on crutches with her casted leg held up behind her.

Genesis had been involved in the case I helped Gina with when I first arrived in town. She was the victim of a hit-and-run. She ended up with a broken leg and a face that was so badly bruised she looked like a loser of an MMA fight. Her face was looking better now. The swelling had gone, and the bruises had turned a puce yellow.

Her recent brush with death had done little to diminish her vibrant fashion sense. She wore a pair of long shorts, a patchwork nightmare. Each vibrant patch had its own unique color. A chaotic quilt that looked like it should be adorning a bed in the Himalayas. Topping off the ensemble was a bright neon green shirt that surprisingly didn't match any of the patches in the pants. She sported a lone yellow tennis shoe on one foot while the other remained enveloped in a cast.

Her blonde hair was feathered in the style of Farrah Fawcett, with several blue streaks.

"Why do you have Wilbur?" Genesis inquired as she reached down to gently stroke the dog's head.

"Dixie went out of town for a few days, so Wilbur is staying with us. This place looks great. When did you decide to expand?"

"The plan has been in the works since I purchased the place, but I never had time. I thought, why not get pampered yourself while your dog does. After the accident, I had to close the shop while I recovered, which was the perfect time to finish the renovations and bring in new staff. Today is our grand opening. I'll introduce you."

She hobbled over to the manicure station, trying

to balance on the rickety crutches.

"Still haven't gotten used to these stupid things. Sydney, this is Hanah."

Hanah glanced up from her nails long enough to give me a brief nod. In her early twenties, she sported more facial piercings than Pinhead. Her earlobes featured large clear rings with a half-inch hole in the center, adding to her edgy appearance.

"Over here..." Genesis said as she limped across the room. "We have Chloe, my hairdresser."

Chloe was in her late twenties with a blonde pixie cut hairstyle.

"Nice to meet you," she said as she moved around the chair and pulled the drape off the customer.

"Same here. My name's Sydney."

"Sydney?" The chair spun around, revealing a familiar figure. The man's face broke into a broad smile. "Girl, it has been way too long since I last saw you." His voice warm and full of genuine excitement.

"Dominic," I replied, a mixture of surprise and joy.

He sprang up from the chair, enveloped me in a warm hug, and planted a kiss on each cheek. I typically avoid physical contact and only give hugs to my family when absolutely necessary, but Dominic was the exception.

We first crossed paths in kindergarten. One day while on the playground we found a small square package wrapped in shiny silver foil. Because of its size we both assumed it was some type of candy and we each wanted it. I remembered our dismay when we opened it up and found a condom inside. Of course, at our age, we didn't know what it was, so we blew it up and played volleyball with it. Dominic and I found ourselves in the principal's office that afternoon, trying to talk ourselves out of detention. Both our moms were summoned to the school, expressing concern and disbelief. That evening, I had to go to confession and meet with sister Catherine. Dominic and I have been best friends ever since.

Dominic had barely changed since high school. His mocha-toned skin seemed flawless. What had once been a thick, unruly mass of woolly hair was now neatly trimmed into a tidy crew cut. He was smartly dressed in khaki pants and a yellow polo shirt. On his feet, he sported stylish loafers, deliberately sans socks. He resembled a young Denzel Washington.

I pulled away from the hug. "I thought you were in Florida visiting your parents?"

"I returned yesterday."

"What are you doing here?"

"I brought Tootles in for a haircut. I figured I might as well get one myself while I was here."

He looked me up and down slowly, the frown tugging at the corners of his mouth making it clear he wasn't completely happy with what he saw.

"You are as gorgeous as ever, but your fashion sense has not improved."

"We can't all keep up with the latest fashion trends."

"Let's find a spot to sit, and you can dish on all that you have been up to since you got back into town. Because sister, I heard you were like a bull in a China shop."

Dominic and I had stayed connected over the years, relying on phone calls and FaceTime to bridge the distance between us. As I recounted all the events from the past month, he listened closely, nodding along and expressing surprise at the twists and turns of my story. However, his reaction was priceless when I shared the tale of the iridescent blue Lucinda. He erupted into laughter, nearly doubling over with amusement as he embraced the ridiculousness of it all.

"I wish I could have seen it," he said, wiping a tear from his eye.

"Maybe we can try it again sometime," I suggested.

"I am sure we can come up with something more... colorful."

I couldn't help but roll my eyes at the pun.

"How are your parents?" Dominic asked.

Dominic was lucky. Several years ago, his parents traded the cold winters for sunny Florida, leaving him in peace to live in their mansion.

"They are still at the farmhouse."

"Does your mother still roll her eyes and click her tongue at you?"

"More like full-blown temper tantrums now."

He gulped. "Sorry I asked."

"Don't be, the doctor said it's menopause."

Dominic winced, his expression shifting with discomfort, and he quickly changed the subject. I guess he didn't want to talk about my mother's hormone changes.

"It's a shame about Mr. McCarthy. He was one of my favorite teachers."

I raised an eyebrow. "Who are you kidding. You hated algebra."

"Yeah, but he never busted me for the pranks I pulled."

I smiled wistfully, recalling my tenth-grade experience. The day of the algebra midterms had arrived, yet I hadn't studied a single page. Instead, I had spent the previous night on a date with Angelo, a basketball player. As I sat at my desk, a cold rush of fear washed over me. I was terrified of failing. Dominic had reassured me, saying not to worry—he would handle it.

I was sweating bullets as I wrote my name on the top of the exam paper. Suddenly, a strange gurgling

17

noise erupted from the sprinkler above my head. I looked up just as a jet of water burst forth. All the sprinklers were activated, and it looked like a spring shower in the room.

I ran out into the hall with the rest of the students to find chaos. The hallway looked like a tropical storm had hit the school. Everyone scrambled for the exits, tripping over each other in a frantic rush for safety. Girls pushed everyone and cried over the loss of their perfect hairdos.

Everyone except Dominic. He stood coolly by my locker, holding an umbrella as if it were the most normal thing in the world. I ducked under the umbrella with him as Mr. McCarthy emerged from his classroom. He looked at us, shook his head, and trudged down the hall, water dripping off his nose.

Dominic was a computer genius. He had hacked the smoke alarm system triggering the sprinklers to go off. The school was shut down for two days, plenty of time for me to study with Dominic's help.

Genesis emerged from the back room with a white poodle on a leash.

"Tootles is done. I'm ready for Wilbur."

She handed the leash to Dominic.

I stood and started to hand Wilbur's leash to Genesis when the front door swung open, causing the bell above the door to jingle.

"I'm here for my pedicure," Lucinda proclaimed with arrogance, waltzing into the room like a queen. She came to a sudden halt in the doorway, her gaze locking onto mine.

"What are you doing here?" she sneered.

Unfazed I replied, "I brought the dog for a haircut."

Lucinda has been my arch nemesis since high school, mostly because I gave her a black eye and a busted ego. A few weeks ago, I also turned her blue. Unfortunately, that had faded, and she was back to her fake golden tan self.

Her lips curled. "No surprise that mangy mongrel belongs to your clan."

I felt my temper flair. "Shouldn't you be getting some silicone injected somewhere?"

Dominic giggled. "Hopefully somewhere other than your breasts. Those girls look like they are ready to explode."

Lucinda's neck turned red, the color creeping up to stain her cheeks a deep pink. "How dare you!" she stuttered as she continued to stand in the doorway, the door gaping wide open.

Out of the corner of my eye, I glimpsed Gina walking down the sidewalk with an Italian sausage sandwich in her hand. The aroma wafted through the air, and Wilbur instantly perked up, tugging on his leash when he smelled the enticing scent. Gina approached Lucinda from behind. Wilbur started to drool. Gina carefully removed the sausage from the bun and discreetly dropped it into Lucinda's purse. I looked at Dominic, who wore an amused smile.

"I am the mayor's wife, and you cannot talk to me that way. I'm going to tell my husband and he-"

Dominic turned, giving me a subtle nod. In unison, we released the leashes, and the moment the restraints went slack, both dogs shot off like cannonballs.

CHAPTER 3

Lucinda's eyes grew large, and then she screamed. She darted out of the door with the dogs hot on her heels. The door clicked shut behind them. I rushed over, yanking the door open, and ran outside, not wanting to miss the spectacle. Lucinda ran about ten feet before stopping, seemingly unaware that the dogs were after her. She screamed again when she turned around and realized she was their target. She took off up the sidewalk, trying to cross the road while the dogs chased her at lightning speed.

The dogs barked furiously, drawing the curious eyes of the pedestrians on the street. When Lucinda was in the middle of the road, a car screeched to a halt just inches from her as the driver blared the horn. Without a moment's hesitation or a single sensible thought, Lucinda sprang onto the car's hood and swiftly climbed onto the roof. She crouched there, panting heavily as she tried to regain her composure, oblivious to her purse that dangled over the edge.

At that moment, Wilbur leaped up and seized the purse with his teeth, tugging relentlessly, as if it were a prize. The sudden jolt nearly sent Lucinda sprawling off the car. Refusing to give up her purse, she ended up in a tug-of-war with the dog.

Tootles stood beside Wilbur, her tail wagging in

excitement as she barked her encouragement. The car driver, clearly agitated, rolled down his window and shouted at Lucinda to get off his car before he called the police. The mere mention of law enforcement had a peculiar way of making them appear as if summoned by magic. Just then, out of the blue, Sean and Blake emerged at our side.

Sean was my brother-in-law, married to my sister, Krista. He held the position of sergeant for the local police department. Blake was the local police detective. Despite standing over six feet tall, with striking features that highlighted his Native American heritage and good looks, we tended to butt heads whenever we met. He was a stickler for the rules and stern about following the law. I on the other hand embraced a more rebellious outlook on life. Believing that many laws were meant to be broken, especially if the intention was justified or the adventure promised excitement. Behind Blake's back, I dubbed him 'Robocop.'

They stood with us as we watched the fight for the purse.

"Are you involved with this in any way?" Blake asked.

"No," Gina, Dominic, and I all replied at the same time.

At long last, the strap of Lucinda's purse gave way with a sudden snap, sending her tumbling backward onto her backside with such unexpected force that she toppled over the side of the car, entirely out of view. The purse soared through the air before landing with a soft thud on the pavement.

Tootles dived into the open purse. With a triumphant snort, she emerged, clutching the sausage between her teeth. Wilbur latched onto the other end, and they ate the sausage, like the dogs in the cartoon. Once they devoured their treat, Gina called out for Wilbur. He came bounding back with Tootles on his tail. He plopped himself down beside Gina, panting happily.

Gina patted him on the head. "That'll do pig. That'll do."

Blake raised an eyebrow in skepticism. "You had nothing to do with this?" There was a hint of disbelief in his tone.

"I can't help it if Lucinda insists on carrying cooked meat in her purse and saunters into a dog grooming shop with it," I replied, desperately trying not to smirk.

At that moment, Lucinda stormed toward us, fury radiating from her. Her hair was a chaotic mess. It was plastered against the side of her head as if she had just emerged from a storm, and a fresh tear marred the knee of her pants.

"This is your fault," she declared, pointing in my direction. "I want her arrested."

"For what?" Sean asked.

"For training that... dog to attack me."

"I met this intimidating dog for the first time this morning. I don't believe that was enough time to train it to do anything." If I thought I could train Wilbur to embarrass Lucinda, I would gladly have devoted an entire night to that mission.

"This is not right," Lucinda exclaimed as she threw her hands in the air in exasperation.

"Why don't you come inside for your pedicure? On the house." Genesis said, swinging the shop door open and inviting her in.

Lucinda huffed, "At least someone appreciates my status. I'll be sure to tell my husband about this." She strolled through the doorway, not giving us a second glance.

As the door swung shut behind her, Genesis let out a breath. "That was the most entertaining thing I've seen in forever," she exclaimed, smiling brightly. "Wilbur's haircut and shampoo will be on the house."

"Thanks," Gina replied, a glimmer of humor in her eyes.

"Well, since there's nothing else to see here, I guess we'll be on our way," Sean said, glancing at Blake with an amused shake of his head as the two of them turned to leave, their laughter trailing behind them.

"That's the best thing I have seen since you punched Lucinda in high school and gave her a black eye." Dominic paused, a look of contemplation crossing his face. "I need a more exciting life," he admitted.

"You should have seen her when she was blue," Gina chimed in.

"Why are you here?" I asked Gina. "I thought I was supposed to meet you at the office after Wilbur's haircut?"

"Walter sent me to fetch you," her tone was casual, but her expression suggested something more. "He wants to talk to you."

"Why me?" I felt a mixture of intrigue and apprehension.

Gina gave me a mischievous grin. "Genesis, can you keep Wilbur until we get back?"

"Of course. Maybe I can scare Lucinda with him."

Wilbur barked his approval. Gina handed Genesis the leash while I said my goodbyes to Dominic, promising to see him soon.

After her service in the Army, Gina decided to channel her few skills and extreme luck into something new and opened 'Gina Hayes Investigations.' She retired after an unfortunate incident caused her to lose most of her hearing in her left ear. She became a PI, much to the disapproval of my mother.

Her office shared a lobby and a receptionist with

'Bordell Law Firm,' a strategic partnership that benefited them both immensely. Many of Gina's cases were referrals from the law office, and the proximity of their offices meant that there was always an investigator on hand to assist with legal matters. Gina would gather information and take photos that they could use in their trials.

As we entered the lobby, the bell above the door chimed, drawing the secretary's attention. Frances was fast approaching her fifties, her hair styled in a towering B52 do, a throwback to the fashion of the 1960s. She was on the phone when we entered but waved to me as we walked through the waiting room.

I trailed behind Gina as we entered the law office. We went down the hallway, the muted thuds of our footsteps filling the space. Gina stopped in front of a closed door to our left. I recognized immediately that this wasn't Walter's office; it was a room I hadn't been in before. With a confident push, Gina swung the door open and stepped inside without knocking, leaving me to wonder what awaited us in this unfamiliar space.

I hesitated outside the door, contemplating what waited within before stepping inside. It was a conference room, dominated by a large rectangular table crafted from dark wood, surrounded by high-backed chairs. The walls were painted light beige, while a solitary framed painting hung on the back wall. The artwork depicted the very building we occupied, dating back to the 1800s when it served as a hospital during the war.

Six people sat at the table. All heads were turned towards me with an air of anticipation that was almost palpable. The only other people in the room I knew were Walter and my sister, Krista.

Not being easily intimidated, I squared my shoulders and nodded to Walter. Walter was seated at the head of the table, his presence commanding as he rose to greet me.

"Sydney, good to see you. Please come in and take a seat."

He gestured to an empty chair positioned between him and Krista. Gina sat at the table directly across from me. A sense of anticipation lingered in the air.

"Sydney this is Sharon Strait." Walter gestured to the woman sitting next to Gina. Sharon had dark wavy hair and a classical round face.

"Next to Sharon is Teresa Kline," he continued.

Teresa was a middle-aged woman with chestnut brown hair and warm brown eyes. She wasn't pretty, but she wasn't unattractive either. Mostly, she was nothing—the kind of person who blends seamlessly into the background.

"These two women are clients of mine," Walter continued.

I gazed at the man sitting next to Krista who had yet to be introduced.

"Mrs. Strait's mother lived at Meadow Springs nursing home. She passed away several weeks ago. Mrs. Strait approached me because she believes her mother's death was not from natural causes."

"Please call me Sharon," she interjected with a smile directed at Walter. She opened a three-ring binder that sat in front of her. "My mother was in perfect health. She only moved to Meadow Springs to escape yard work, and she was lonely and wanted to live around people her own age."

"Meadow Spring is designed for independent seniors, each residing in their own private one-bedroom apartment," Krista explained. Krista was interning at the law office and would be a fully licensed attorney soon.

Sharon's voice pierced the air. "Someone in that building murdered my mother."

The man seated next to Krista responded calmly. "Mrs. Strait, I assure you my employees are trained professionals. You know that they found out that your mother's blood sugar was too low. That's what caused her ultimate demise."

I leaned forward in my chair so I could see around Krista and get a better look at the man who was speaking. He was dressed in a tailored navy suit. I noticed him tugging at his collar like a man loosening the noose before facing his execution.

"My mother did not accidentally overdose on her insulin. She was meticulous about taking care of her blood sugar." Sharon declared, her voice laced with underlying fury. Sharon stood and slammed her palms down on the table. "One of your employees or residents killed her."

"Enough." Walter's voice boomed. "We agreed this would be a civilized meeting."

Sharon's face flushed with embarrassment, and she sank back down into her chair. The man's face started turning red, and he loosened his tie.

"Sydney, Sharon had her mother's blood tested for the sugar level."

Sharon flipped through a few pages in her binder. "I wanted a complete autopsy report," she said with frustration. "But they flat-out refused. I was told there wasn't enough evidence to prove foul play."

As thick as the binder was, she must have had a complete record of her mother's life since birth. Walter cleared his throat and looked pointedly at Sharon, obviously not liking the interruption.

"Teresa's mother died about a month ago at the same facility. She also believes her mother's death was not from natural causes."

Teresa sat quietly at the table. Her eyes downcast "This is Mr. Thomas York," Walter said gesturing at the man sitting next to Krista. "He is the CEO of the retirement community and a personal acquaintance of mine."

"Naturally, I find no reason to suspect that these two deaths were anything but natural," Mr. York's gaze shifted to Sharon.

Her lips were tightly puckered and her brow was furrowed. She looked like she was fighting back the urge to jump over the table and choke him.

"However, the patients' health and safety are our number one concern. I will personally take measures to ensure the quality of care our facility provides."

Sharon let out a derisive scoff, unimpressed by his polished speech.

Walter leaned back in his chair. "Teresa has made the decision to exhume her mother's remains and have an autopsy. She believes it will unveil the true cause of her mother's death. The required paperwork has been signed, and we can expect approval within the next few days."

I leaned back, my gaze fixed on Mr. York. His complexion had taken on a ghostly pale green, an unsettling shade that hinted at his unease. I couldn't tell if his color change was a response to the gruesome thought of retrieving a lifeless body from the earth or if it stemmed from anxiety about the impending autopsy results. Based on his skin's deepening green, I was going with the former.

"I encouraged Teresa to have her mother removed and autopsied. Maybe then we can find out the truth." Sharon said smugly.

She most likely steamrolled Teresa into being part of this whole thing. I wondered if Teresa truly believed her mother was murdered.

"How did your mother die?" Gina asked Teresa.

"Her name was Evaline. She had heart problems. They said she had a heart attack." Teresa's voice was barely above a whisper. "She was at the doctor's the day before she passed away and he said she was doing great and her heart would last another five years. When Sharon started talking about her mother's death, I started thinking about my mom and wondering if her death was from fowl play too."

Sharon's grin stretched across her face, reminding me of a Cheshire cat.

"This is an interesting story, but I don't quite understand why I'm here." I glanced at Gina, whose unsettling grin made the hairs on my neck stand up. I began to wonder if I was going to regret joining them.

Walter rose from his seat and strode to a small corner refrigerator with a coffee pot atop it.

"Sydney, would you like something to drink?"

"Water would be nice."

He opened the fridge with a soft whoosh, revealing a neatly organized interior glistening with chilled items. From the cool depths, he retrieved a bottle of Evian water and handed it to me with a casual gesture. I fought to mask my surprise at the sight of such luxurious water—something I wasn't accustomed to, as my usual source was the tap.

Unscrewing the cap, I lifted the bottle to my lips and swallowed, expecting a burst of refreshing flavor. Instead, I was met with the same familiar taste of water I always knew, leaving me somewhat disappointed considering the cost of this particular brand of water.

"Thomas and I have discussed this case," he continued, shifting back to the matter at hand, his tone suddenly serious. "He has agreed to allow us to send someone to infiltrate the nursing facility. This person would take on the role of a new employee."

A chill ran down my spine and my throat felt like sandpaper. I took another swallow of the cold water.

"Since most of my employees are nurses. Gina

suggested you as the best person for the job," Thomas said.

I started coughing, choking on my water. Krista patted me on the back several times. When I could breathe again, I rose to my feet, flashing an irritated glance at Gina.

"Can I speak to you in the hall," I croaked.

Sharon and Teresa exchanged glances.

Walter's brow furrowed in confusion. "Is everything alright?"

"Yes, I just need to talk to Gina."

Gina hadn't moved from the chair yet so I gave her an 'I will shoot you if you don't move' look. She rose and walked over to the door where I pushed her into the hall. With a resounding thud, I closed the door behind us.

As soon as the click of the latch echoed in the silence, I confronted her, my frustration bubbling to the surface. "Are you out of your mind?" I exclaimed, unable to contain the exasperation in my voice.

"I don't see what the problem is."

I sighed deeply, raising my hand and waving it in front of her face to ensure she was paying attention.

"Hello?" I said, my voice firm. "I'm not a nurse. I pretend to be a nurse, remember? I don't even know how to take a temperature."

"They don't know that."

My mouth fell open. She could not be serious.

"I'm NOT a nurse," I replied, trying to maintain my composure.

"You're a spy."

"No," I corrected her. "I'm an intelligence agent."

With an exaggerated wave of her hand, she dismissed me. "Same difference. You go undercover all the time. This case isn't any different. Besides, you've had medical training."

"Yeah, for big emergencies like applying a

tourniquet to a severed limb or stopping a bullet wound from bleeding out. That's hardly the same as nursing." I closed my eyes and rubbed my temple. "What if they want me to use a stethoscope? Or worse," I said, looking up with a hint of panic in my eyes. "What if I see an old person's butt."

Gina chuckled. "They mentioned the residents are independent, so there won't be much actual work involved, and knowing the word stethoscope has to count for something."

"And seeing old people's butts?"

"That's just an added bonus," she said with a twinkle in her eyes. "So, are you in?"

I gave her the finger.

"Good." She opened the door to the conference room, ending our conversation.

The only sound echoing through the room was the steady hum of the air conditioner. All eyes in the room were fixed on us expectantly. Gina gave them a confident thumbs-up. A wave of relief washed over the group as I returned to my seat.

Walter leaned forward, resting his elbows on the table and steepling his fingers. "Excellent."

"I do have a few concerns," I said, casting a sharp glare at Gina, who gave me a bright smile. I kicked her in the shin effectively erasing it.

"I'm home on leave with injuries, so I hope this won't be too strenuous."

"Not at all. I have talked to Thomas about this already and we have devised a plan," Walter replied.

"Yes," Thomas continued. "I going to tell my staff that you just had a baby and are only looking to work a few hours a week for extra money."

A light giggle escaped Krista's lips, catching her off guard before she quickly composed herself. In stark contrast, Gina couldn't contain herself. She burst into laughter, her amusement so great that she snorted. It was nice to know I wasn't the only one who thought that my having a child was absurd.

"Anyways, you'll be training with our head nurse Shirley. She primarily handles the paperwork and scheduling."

I internally sighed in relief. Good no butts.

"Just keep a close eye on the nurses and residents, and report back to me if anything seems off," Walter instructed.

I nodded. Krista gave my shoulder a gentle squeeze, offering her support.

"Great, both women passed away in the evening, so we'd like you to start your shift tomorrow night around six."

Thomas flung his briefcase on the table. He flipped it open and retrieved a vanilla-colored folder. He handed it to Krista, who passed it on to me.

"Inside, you will find the address and the layout of the building. I've also included pertinent information about the employees and the current residents of the home. My business card is stapled to the front of the folder with my personal cellphone number. Call me day or night if you require assistance."

Thomas rose from his seat signaling the conclusion of our meeting. He walked around Krista's chair, shook my hand, and left the room.

"Make sure to keep an eye on everyone. Something's not right in that place," Sharon said as she headed for the door where Teresa was waiting. Walter gave a brief nod before exiting the room. The rest of us walked across the hall to Krista's office.

I flopped down in one of the two chairs facing her desk. With a heavy sigh, I leaned my head back, staring up at the ceiling. "I can't believe you dragged me into this."

Krista perched on the edge of her desk and leaned close with concern etched on her face. "Are you still in a lot of pain? Maybe it's too early for you to be working again."

Gina and I exchanged a knowing glance. No one knew me better than Krista, and for good reason. Not only was she my sister, but she was also my twin. Luckily, we didn't share similar looks, but we still had a twin connection.

I had kept my secret away from my family, unwilling to burden them with the weight of my truth. So, I had crafted a facade, telling them I was an Army nurse. They accepted it, picturing me as a flight nurse soaring through the skies on a helicopter. Only Gina and our grandfather, Pap, knew the reality of my existence. Internationally, I pursued drug dealers, terrorists, and other nefarious individuals.

My father had suspicions but remained silent, likely because of the chaos that would ensue if my mother discovered the truth. She was already overwhelmed by menopause, her relentless worry about my love life, and her constant attempts to play matchmaker for me. If she learned how dangerous my true job was, it would undoubtedly push her over the edge of sanity. The aftermath might force my dad to move in with Pap, seeking refuge from her meltdown.

When I arrived in town, I spun a tale to everyone, claiming that I had taken a tumble down a flight of stairs, leaving me with broken ribs. Being gunned down during a drug raid didn't seem to be the appropriate story to tell my family. I could just picture their reaction. They would wrap me in bubble wrap and confine me to the cellar.

"No, my ribs haven't been hurting much," I said.

"Are you scared? I would be. If there's been a murder, that place could be dangerous," Krista said.

"Hmmph," Gina stifled a laugh. She was fully

aware of my extensive training and the formidable adversaries I had encountered. Individuals that would make a small-town killer look as dangerous as a kitten.

"I'm fine. I was just enjoying my vacation," I lied.

To be honest, during the first few days indulging in the luxury of doing nothing was nice. I would relax on the front porch swing and watch the world float by or catch up on television and news. But soon, the novelty wore thin, boredom settled in, and I grew antsy.

At first, I had paced the house. Eventually, I cleaned every nook and cranny of the entire house right down to the pantry. I even alphabetized the spices, a task that felt absurd considering Gina never cooked.

Gina's purse erupted in a fit of giggling, sounding like a group of teenage girls. She rummaged through the bag, pulling out her phone and checking the text.

"Genesis is done with Wilbur."

Krista nodded. "Why don't I order a pizza from Antonio's? We can meet at Gina's for dinner and review the information in the file."

We all agreed. Gina and I left to pick up the dog. As we walked to her car, I couldn't believe I let her talk me into this. A sinking feeling settled in my stomach. I was sure this was going to be trouble.

CHAPTER 4

With his fresh haircut and bath, Wilbur finally resembled a dog. He didn't remind me of any particular breed, more like a Heinz 57. He had big brown eyes and a cold, black, wet nose that he eagerly nudged against my arm in hopes I would pet him.

The moment we stepped through the front door, his excitement was palpable. He scampered over to the kitchen and scratched at the back door, a chorus of barks escaping his mouth. Hearing that sound, Cagney and Lacey flocked up to the door. I swung it open, and with a joyful leap, Wilbur bounded outside, ready to play with his new friends.

Meanwhile, the rich, slightly caramelized aroma filled the kitchen as I removed the lid from a can of coffee. I poured the dark, fragrant grounds into the top of the coffee pot without a second thought, knowing that I preferred my brew strong. After pressing the button to start the brew, I leaned against the counter, savoring the anticipation. Nothing was more heavenly than a fresh cup of coffee or a good rum.

I poured myself a steaming cup of hot coffee, but before I could enjoy the first taste, Krista strolled into the room and snatched the cup from my hand. She settled herself at the table and kicked off her shoes with a sigh of relief. I poured two more cups and sat at the table, where Gina joined us. Krista crossed one leg over the other and started to massage her toes.

"I couldn't wait to get those shoes off," she declared.

"If you hate them so much, throw them out," I suggested.

Her eyes widened. "They're six-hundred-dollar Valentinos."

My jaw dropped in disbelief. "You paid six hundred dollars for a single pair of shoes." I was sure every piece of clothing I owned combined didn't come close to that price.

"I'm going to be a lawyer soon. I have to dress the part."

Just then, the doorbell rang. Gina pushed herself from the table and walked briskly to the door. A moment later, she returned, balancing a large pizza box and a delivery bag, the delicious aroma wafting through the air.

My stomach instantly started growling as I smelled the cheesy pie. I eagerly flipped open the pizza box, the steam escaping in tiny curls. I snatched a piece greedily. I took a large bite and sighed in content.

"You're easy to please," Gina remarked as she removed a salad from the plastic bag.

"What is that?" I said, distaste dripping from my voice.

I knew the professionals preached about well-balanced meals, but to me, pizza was the quintessential food. It had everything—bread, dairy in the form of cheese, and meat if you added the pepperoni. It also contained a vegetable or fruit, depending on whether they ever decided what a tomato was.

"Don't worry, the salad is for me," Gina said. "I'm on a diet."

Krista looked a little scared. "Uh oh."

"What's that for?" Gina asked as she took a bite of spinach and cringed. She chewed slowly, clearly unimpressed.

"Last time you were on a diet, you sucked the cookie dough directly from the tube," I said.

"Not all of us are blessed with your metabolism. Just wait, one day when you eat chocolate, it will go straight to your hips too."

I chuckled. "You're only seven years older than me. You're not ancient yet."

My grandparents had Gina late in life, so even though she was my aunt, she was more like a big sister.

"It's not like you to diet. Something else is going on," Krista said.

We both fixed our gazes on Gina, waiting for her to crack.

"Fine. I have a date tomorrow night," she blurted out before shoveling another forkful of rabbit food into her mouth.

"Who?" Krista asked with excitement, jumping up and down.

"No one you know," Gina said as she avoided eye contact and focused intently on her plate.

I watched her closely, my mind racing as I tried to recall moments she might have interacted with a new guy. I had almost always been at her side and didn't remember her talking to anyone new. Then, like a bolt from the blue, the realization struck me.

"Oh my God. You're online dating."

A blush crept into Gina's cheeks, and she crossed her arms defiantly. "We aren't here to discuss my dating life. Let's focus on the case."

Krista tossed her pizza crust onto the lid of the half-empty box. "Fine, but we're coming back to this later."

She opened the folder Thomas had handed over, its pages filled with case notes and details, and began scanning the documents. "We have two women who believe their mothers were murdered in the building they lived in. One of them died from an insulin overdose, and the other from a heart attack."

Gina leaned in closer, her brow furrowing in thought. "I suppose the first question we need answered is whether either woman had company the night they died."

Krista shrugged as she flipped a page. "That is something Sydney will need to investigate when she's there. Given that their deaths were ruled as natural causes, there's not much else to go on. Thomas wants to avoid raising suspicion among the staff, so you must ask your questions carefully and discreetly."

"We also need to identify the employees on duty those two nights. That would help narrow down the suspects," Gina suggested.

I tapped my fingernail against the coffee cup. "I wonder who else has died at Meadow Springs lately? It could be connected."

"Maybe you could speak to a few residents and see what they might know."

I sighed. "It's going to be impossible for me to sneak around and ask questions while pretending to do my actual job."

We fell silent, contemplating the complexity of the situation.

Krista suddenly straightened, an idea sparking in her eyes. "What if I call Thomas? I could see if he could hire Gina as a housekeeper or maybe a volunteer, anything that would provide a legitimate reason for her to be there. Two people digging for information could reveal much more than just one."

"That's a great idea," Gina agreed.

Krista's phone erupted with 'All of Me' by John Legend.

Gina and I exchanged glances, our eyes sparkling

with amusement as Krista talked on the phone.

"It's Sean," she announced cheerfully, her expression brightening. "He's finally home for the first evening in over a week." A hint of excitement danced in her eyes as she ended the call. "Sorry to dash, but I'll fill you in tomorrow."

"To be young and in love," Gina said, her eyes turning glossy.

"I want to hear about your date for tomorrow night," I said.

"Later. Let's take this dinner into the living room and see if we can find a medical show to watch. Maybe you can learn some terminology that will be helpful for you tomorrow."

She made her way to the back door. She gave an ear-piercing whistle, and Wilbur came running in, dirt rolling off his nose and onto the floor.

"Look at him. His nose and front paws are covered in dirt, and he just had a bath today," I said.

"Guess he's been busy digging in the yard." Taking a dishrag, she washed his face and paw.

Once Wilbur returned to his clean self, we retreated into the living room and settled in for a quiet night.

* * * *

The following day, I was stirred awake by rain slapping against my bedroom window. The air was filled with an inviting blend of sweet almond and vanilla. I rolled over onto my stomach, momentarily questioning if I was still in a dream. I took a deep breath and confirmed that the room smelled like a bakery mingled with a hint of coffee. It was a strange smell for this house since neither Gina nor I prepared such delightful treats.

I quickly put on my Khaki cargo shorts and

matching T-shirt and laced up my sturdy, worn boots.

With a practiced motion, I retrieved my gun from beneath the pillow, the cold steel sending a familiar chill through my fingertips. I slipped it into the waistband at my back, wincing slightly at the unwelcome bite of the metal against my skin; after all these years of carrying it, you'd think I'd be used to the cool touch of the weapon.

As I opened my bedroom door, I was taken aback to see Gina emerge from her room, rubbing the sleep from her eyes. She was wearing pink pajamas adorned with monkeys.

She looked as surprised to find me still upstairs as I was to see her. "Did you go to the bakery this morning?"

I shook my head, dashed down the stairs, bursting into the kitchen. I stopped dead in my tracks at the site in front of me.

Dominic stood confidently at the stove, clad in a white chef's hat. His apron was designed with a muscled Greek god flaunting a speedo. In one hand, he wielded a spatula like a maestro wielding a baton.

"The coffee is ready," he said as he flipped something sizzling in the pan.

"What are you doing here?"

"Making breakfast. I've made crepes stuffed with strawberries, cream cheese, and almond croissants."

Gina strolled in, her eyes lighting up at the sight of the spread. She picked up a croissant and tore off the crispy end, savoring the satisfying crunch before popping it into her mouth. "This is heavenly," she exclaimed, her voice muffled through her first bite. "Where's Wilbur?"

"I left him outside when I came in," Dominic replied.

Some watchdog. I walked over to the door to inspect the lock.

"How did you get in?" I asked.

"The backdoor was unlocked," Dominic replied

casually, using the spatula to slide a crepe from the sizzling pan onto a plate. He picked up the plate and took a seat at the table. He dolloped a swirl of whipped cream onto his crepe with a spoon.

"You don't lock your door at night?" I asked Gina.

"It's a quiet neighborhood," she shrugged. "Nothing ever happens."

"I'm sure Charles Manson's victims thought the same thing."

Gina stuck her tongue out at me.

I eased open the back door and leaned against the frame, keenly observing through the screen. My eyes were drawn to the far corner of the property where a small, weathered shed stood. Gina had shared that the previous owner had transformed it into a makeshift chicken coop after her husband had walked out on her.

Despite the steady drizzle, Wilbur and the chicken energetically dug in the damp earth near the coop. I could only imagine what they were up to. I turned away and headed to the table, ready to savor breakfast.

* * * *

"I can't eat another bite," I declared as I forked the last piece of crepe into my mouth.

Gina let out a satisfied burp. "I know. I'm going to skip eating the rest of the day."

"Don't you have a date tonight?" I asked.

"He works late, so we're not meeting at the restaurant until seven-thirty. That's plenty of time to digest my breakfast."

Dominic dabbed at his mouth with a crisp white napkin as he finished his breakfast. We gathered our plates and started cleaning up the kitchen. I offered to wash the dishes while Gina cleared the table. It had stopped raining during breakfast, and now the golden rays of sunlight were trying to break through the clouds, promising another beautiful day.

As I loaded the last dish in the dishwasher, an ear-piercing howl penetrated the tranquility of the morning. It was followed by the frantic clucking of the chickens.

"What on earth are they doing out there?" Gina asked.

"They were digging near the side of the shed earlier," I replied as we gathered around the screen door, peering into the yard.

Wilbur and Cagney were locked in a tug-of-war, each gripping the end of something that dangled precariously between their mouths. Their feet dug into the soft earth as they pulled with all their might, determined to claim their prize.

"Look at that hole next to the coop," Gina exclaimed, exasperation lacing her voice. "Were they trying to dig to China?"

The old screen door creaked in protest as we stepped outside into the backyard, drawn by the ruckus. When the screen door banged against the house, Lacey peered over the edge of the hole.

She glanced up at us briefly before ducking back into the ground. Cagney flapped her wings, catching Wilbur completely off guard. Taking advantage of his hesitation, she ripped the object of desire out of his mouth with a triumphant squawk and darted across the yard, a flash of feathers and mischief.

Wilbur, in full pursuit, lunged after her, and a chase erupted. The yard was modest in size, allowing them to loop in circles around the three of us as we stood in quiet amusement. With his four sturdy legs, Wilbur was quick and determined, gradually closing the gap as he nipped playfully at Cagney's tail feathers. Just as he seemed about to catch her, Cagney would flap her wings, elevating herself about a foot into the air, skillfully evading his grasp.

After several trips around us, Cagney must have gotten tired because she flew up and perched on Gina's shoulder like a parrot. Wilbur sat at Gina's feet, barking, his gaze fixed on the bird.

"What's in her mouth?" I asked.

The object protruding from Cagney's mouth was white and measured about three inches long.

"It looks like a bone," Dominic said in disgust.

Gina reached up and tugged the object from Cagney's mouth. Sure enough, we could see it was a small, weathered bone. Cagney let out a low growl in protest before she leapt off Gina's shoulder.

"Do you think they got it from that hole they dug?" Gina asked, glancing at the freshly disturbed earth nearby.

"Maybe a dead cat or squirrel," I replied, curiosity pulling me towards the hole.

"Oh, gross. You go ahead. I'll wait right here," Dominic said.

"Ha. You don't want to see a dead animal?" I teased as I approached the dark opening in the ground.

"No, thank you," he said crossing his arms over his chest.

Lacey poked her head out of the hole once more. When she noticed us approaching, she flew away.

"Suit yourself," I said.

Gina and I leaned closer to the edge of the hole, our gazes locked in a moment of shared surprise that must have shown on our faces.

Dominic chimed in. "What kind of dead animal is it?"

Gina and I exchanged tense glances. "It's not an animal," I said as I knelt at the hole's edge.

"The suspense is killing me," Dominic said as he

strolled over to us and tentatively investigated the hole. "It's just a dirty old boot," he said, his eyebrows raised in disbelief.

In the middle of the nine-inch-deep cavity lay an old, battered black leather boot resting unceremoniously on its side. The leather was cracking, and the seams were beginning to unravel. Judging by its size, it was unmistakably a man's boot.

I picked the boot out of the hole and stood up, bringing it to eye level. What I found interesting was that even though the laces were threadbare, they were tied in a neat bow.

"How often does someone tie the laces on a shoe unless they are wearing it?" I said, studying the boot for a moment, before I turned it upside down and shook it.

Several small brittle bones tumbled out of the boot, clanking together as they hit the ground.

"What kind of bones are they?" Dominic inquired.

Gina's expression tightened, her apprehension evident as she looked at the bones.

"Foot bones," I murmured with a heavy sigh, knowing this was not good.

CHAPTER 5

As we awaited the arrival of the police, I set the worn boot on the ground beside the scattered bones. After our call, Sean pulled up to the house quickly with Blake following closely behind. Settling into the lawn chairs, I could feel the tension in the air, a silent acknowledgment of the scene unfolding before us.

"Whose foot do you think was in the boot?" Dominic asked, breaking the silence.

A deeper concern gnawed at me. "The big question is where is the rest of him." Our gazes were instinctively drawn to the shed, its door hanging ajar.

"Is the floor concrete?" I asked. The muted gray color suggested a solid foundation, one that could easily conceal more than just tools.

Gina nodded.

Dominic clapped. "This is exciting. We just found a dead guy's foot."

"Maybe, it's just a foot. The guy it belongs to could still be alive," Gina reasoned.

"Seriously," I said to Gina knowing neither of us believed the person the foot belonged to was still alive. I turned towards Dominic. "A minute ago, you were squeamish about finding a dead animal. Now you're excited about finding a body part."

"A lot of people find dead animals. No one ever

finds dead bodies. This is a great story to tell people."

I had to disagree with that statement. Just last month Gina and I found a dead body.

We sipped our chilled iced tea as several other police officers filed through the gate. They methodically bagged the boot and skeletal remains. Dominic got bored and decided it was time to go home.

Meanwhile, one of the newer officers knelt beside the grave, carefully probing the dirt. After a moment, he shook his head. I guess that was all the bones that lay hidden in the dark earth. I was so focused on the unfolding scene that I didn't notice someone else entering the yard until he stalked up to Blake.

He was stocky, nearly a head shorter than Blake. A sparse patch of black hair was meticulously combed over his balding scalp, the feeble tufts standing in stark contrast to the smoothness of his head. How could anyone believe that those long, thin strands could ever create the illusion of a full head of hair?

I looked at Gina questioningly.

"That's the sheriff, Earl Hendersen," she said.

"Why haven't we seen him before?" I asked, my voice laced with curiosity. Just a few weeks prior, Gina and I had stumbled upon a body sprawled on the floor of his office. It had been a particularly brutal week, with two murder victims discovered in the same period, yet the sheriff had seemed strangely absent.

"He and his wife were on a cruise in the Bahamas. I heard they just returned yesterday."

After a lengthy discussion with Blake, the sheriff barked out some orders. Sean left the yard carrying the baggies with the boot and bones. Once Sean was out of sight, the sheriff pivoted on his heel, his beady eyes narrowing as they fixed intently on us.

"Uh, oh," Gina whispered.

I didn't understand her concern. After all, she

didn't bury the foot in the backyard. If she ever decided to kill someone, she would set them on fire or blow them up in a car explosion.

"Ms. Hayes," the sheriff said in a deep authoritative tone.

"Yes," we both answered in unison.

The sheriff glanced back and forth between us, his expression a mix of frustration and disappointment. He pursed his lips, clearly unamused.

"We are going to have to tear down the shed," he declared. "Blake has already contacted a construction crew to handle it."

Gina sprang to her feet. "You can't just do that! Where will my chickens live?"

He raised his hand, palm facing her. "That's not my concern," he replied, his tone flat and dismissive. "The rest of the body may be under that shed, and we need to find out. End of discussion."

Gina's bottom lip jutted out in a defiant pout. I felt my spine stiffen.

"You could be a little nicer about it," I snapped.

His lips pressed into a thin line. "It's not my job to be nice. You must be Sydney. I've heard quite a bit about you."

"All good things, I'm sure." I glanced at Blake, who shrugged in response, his expression unreadable.

"That I cannot say. I came over to inform you that I'm back in town."

I couldn't help but offer him a sardonic smile. "How wonderful of you to grace us with your presence and point out the obvious. Rest assured, the offensive cloud of your cologne had already made your presence clear."

His face flushed a deep crimson, the color spreading so rapidly that I half-expected his head to explode with anger. "They don't pay me enough to put up with people like you. I'm warning you to stay out of this investigation. I heard about your meddling in the last case, and that won't fly while I'm in charge. If I even catch a whisper of your involvement, I'll throw you in jail. Do you understand?" His gaze pierced through us like a knife.

Sometimes, the amount of self-control it took not to say what was on my mind was so intense I felt the urge to scream into a pillow, or worse, shoot someone. My fingers were just itching to try the latter.

In an effort to contain my composure, I saluted him and replied sarcastically, "Yes sir."

The vein in his forehead started to bulge out. "Don't get smart with me, girlie," he spat, flecks of saliva flying from his mouth. "Your aunt has caused nothing but trouble since she arrived in town. You both need to stay away." He whirled around and marched away, disappearing around the side of the house.

"And I thought you were bad," I said, addressing Blake.

A flicker of amusement danced in his eyes. "So I've heard," he replied, a smirk tugging at his lips. "I guess Robocop doesn't seem so bad after all."

I couldn't help but chuckle. "He's more of an insufferable as-"

Gina interrupted. "Don't take it personally. He's still angry with me."

"Why?" I asked, fully aware that my curiosity might lead me to regret the answer.

"It all started at the chili cook-off last spring," Blake said. A hint of a smile tugged at his lips.

Gina threw her hands in the air. "I was simply demonstrating a faster way to light the charcoal in his grill."

"How?" I found myself unable to resist asking.

"With a little gunpowder."

"A bit too much gunpowder," Blake replied. "I was several grills away and all I heard was a 'whoomph."

"What happened next?" I asked.

"Burnt off both his eyebrows. His face looked sunburned for days," Blake said as his mouth curved into a smile.

I couldn't help but laugh.

"He was such a baby about it." Gina said. "You would have thought I cut off his arm. He hasn't liked me since."

"I need to return to the station. Officer Craig will stay here to oversee things, and the construction crew will arrive shortly. Sorry about the shed," Blake said, following the sheriff's steps around the house.

"So, gunpowder huh?" I chuckled.

Gina crossed her arms over her chest. "I don't want to talk about it."

* * * *

We spent the remainder of the afternoon observing a group of construction workers as they tore down the old shed. The air was filled with a rhythmic thudding as they jackhammered the concrete base.

Gina sighed, "Why can't construction workers look like the ones you see in commercials? You know, all muscular, sweaty, and shirtless."

I chuckled as my gaze landed on a particular hairy-armed middle-aged man with a generous beer belly. When he bent over, he displayed his plumber's crack which was so pronounced it made the Grand Canyon look small. "I could go out there and ask them to take their shirts off for you."

Gina followed my gaze, her lip curling in disgust as she took in the sight before us. "No, thank you."

After a while, she rested her head on the table, her

49

eyelids fluttering as fatigue overtook her. Eventually, I nudged her with my elbow to wake her up.

"What?" She yawned and stretched her arms above her head.

"Something's going on."

The construction crew had pried up the concrete slab. A small excavator, its bright yellow paint chipped and worn, was busy clawing away at the earth. However, after only a few passes, the machine suddenly ground to a halt. The driver, a short man with a hard hat positioned on his head, sprang out of the cab and rushed over to the police officer standing nearby. The officer bent down to peer into the gaping hole, his brow furrowing. He spoke intently into the radio clipped to his shoulder, a serious look etched on his face.

"They must have found something," Gina said with excitement.

"Or someone," I replied.

Not long after the call, Blake and Sean arrived in the backyard. Sean gripped a heavy equipment box in his hand. He jumped into the shallow hole. They all worked together and eventually lifted out a black body bag.

"Guess that answers our question," I said.

Blake jumped out of the hole and dusted himself off.

His eyes locked onto the house as he began striding purposefully towards it. He reached the back screen door and gave it a solid knock. Gina swung the door open to let him inside.

"I have a few questions for you, Gina," Blake said, his tone serious and inquisitive.

"We figured," I said.

We relayed our findings to Blake during his initial visit, detailing how we stumbled upon the boot and the remnant bones.

"How long has that shed been there?"

"I don't know. I bought the property about a year ago, and it was already there when I moved in."

"Do you know who the previous owner was?" he inquired.

"Mini West sold me the place."

His eyebrow shot up. "Mini West? As in the wife of Charles West?"

Gina shrugged, "I suppose so."

"What's so intriguing about Charles West?" I asked.

"He was the old coroner. A couple of years ago he vanished. The talk was he left town with his mistress." He shifted his gaze to address Gina again. "Do you have any idea where Mini is now?"

"She told me that she was selling the house to move into an apartment, but she didn't say where."

"Thanks for your help," Blake replied before making his exit.

I watched his figure retreat, the door clicking shut behind him, before voicing my concerns. "Do you think Charles has truly left, or could he possibly be the body buried under the shed?"

"I don't know," Gina replied. "But we'll need to find out where Mini is and talk to her about it."

I pulled a water bottle from the fridge. "Do you have a gun safe in the house?"

"No, why do you ask?"

"I have a few firearms stashed away in my duffle bag. If someone were to break in through the door you keep unlocked ..." I gave her a pointed stare. "Or if the police need to search the house for any reason, I wouldn't want them to discover them."

Nurses typically don't carry around an arsenal when they travel.

"I have something better," Gina declared as she strolled into the pantry. Curious, I set my water bottle down on the counter and followed her.

She stood on her tiptoes in the pantry, reaching for something high above. She stretched for the next-to-top shelf at the back of the pantry, where her fingertips grazed the largest can of Spam I had ever seen. The thought of that gelatinous block of meat sliding onto my dinner plate sent a wave of nausea through me.

Gina laughed at my expression. "Yea, I think most people feel that way about Spam," she said as she picked up the can.

Suddenly, a sharp click echoed in the room, and a small panel on the back wall shifted, revealing a narrow opening. Gina tugged at the concealed panel, which swung open to unveil a hidden compartment. My jaw dropped in astonishment. Gina stepped aside, inviting me to peer into the space beyond the wall.

The dimly lit room featured a wall adorned with a few handguns. In one corner, a weathered wooden box, with a black skull and crossbones painted on it, laid open, its lid ajar. Inside, neatly arranged sticks of dynamite laid with a handful of grenades thrown in. Next to this unsettling sight was a rusted metal tin, its faded paint proclaiming 'gun powder' in stark white letters.

Scattered throughout the shadowy cubby were several gallon-sized jugs filled with clear liquid, which scared me. What could possibly be in those jugs that warranted the need for them to be stored in a hidden cubby hole? I decided it was best not to ask. Even more unsettling were the four brick-sized blocks of grimy white clay.

"Is that C4?"

Gina averted her gaze. "Maybe."

I looked up to study the ceiling.

"What are you doing?" she asked.

"Trying to determine the distance of my bedroom from this death trap."

Her smile was not reassuring. "Be realistic. If this room blows up, it'll take out the entire block."

That was comforting.

"You know, for someone who defused bombs for a living, you sure have a lot of explosive devices."

She gave me a wink. "I have to have some fun."

I shook my head and continued to scan the area. My attention was drawn to an ancient wooden crate in the corner.

Inside, I discovered a collection of a dozen glass bottles, their surfaces encrusted with cobwebs and coated in at least a century's worth of dust. I carefully lifted one of the bottles from the crate and blew most of the dust off it. The dust swirled up into a cloud and landed on Gina causing her to cough and sneeze.

"Sorry," I said.

The bottle's label was gold, with a silhouette of a black horse on it. "Old Hickory Bourbon," I read. "Bottled 1926."

Gina nodded, "I suspected this space was created during prohibition to hide their illicit alcohol."

"How did you manage to open it?"

"There is a pressure lever under the can of spam. When I first moved in, I discovered a can of lard that seemed as old as the house itself. I doubt the previous owners ever bothered to move it. When I went to throw it out, it was sitting on the lever, and I found this room. I decided to replace that can with something no one ever wants to eat."

"This place is perfect. Let me get my guns."

* * * *

It was early evening when Krista arrived to assist Gina and me in preparing for our undercover mission at Meadow Springs. She handed me a shopping bag, and I pulled out a set of lilac-purple scrubs.

"You're kidding, right?" I exclaimed.

"You're a nurse. You have to wear scrubs," Krista said.

I arched an eyebrow.

"What color scrubs do you normally wear?"

I thought quickly. "Black," I remembered one nurse wearing black scrubs during my hospital stay.

"Figures."

Gina bounded down the stairs with infectious energy. She wore well-fitted jeans and a plain gray T-shirt that clung comfortably to her frame.

"Why doesn't she have to wear scrubs?" I asked.

"Because she's part of housekeeping."

As I watched Gina, it struck me that her role seemed much easier than mine. I had this feeling I wouldn't like this mission, and deep down, I knew I wouldn't enjoy what lay ahead.

CHAPTER 6

We pulled into Meadow Springs just before five o'clock. The building loomed large before us, its U-shaped structure rising two stories high, clad in tan vinyl siding that reflected the soft light of early evening. As we circled to the rear of the building, we spotted a solitary gray door marked by a sign that read "Employee Entrance."

We entered through the door and followed the corridor until we found an open office with a woman sitting behind the desk. She was dressed completely in white, including her sneakers. When she noticed us, she looked up from the computer screen with a warm smile that illuminated her face.

"Can I help you?" she inquired.

"My name's Sydney. I'm supposed to start training today."

"And I'm Gina."

"How did you get in here?" She asked as she sifted through the disorganized stack of paperwork on her desk.

"The back door was open, so we came in," I replied.

She frowned. "I keep telling T.J. to relock the door after he comes in. He's always forgetting."

She pulled a paper from the stack. "Ah Gina, here

you are. My name's Shirley Stahl, and I'm the charge nurse for this shift. It says here you are our new housekeeper."

Gina nodded.

"Your shift is only for a couple of hours. You need to clean the dining room and vacuum the halls." She gestured towards the corridor. "Go back down to the first door on your left. That's the supply closet. The residents just finished dinner, so you can start cleaning the dining room. After you gather your supplies, head down the hallway. The dining room is in the middle of the building."

Gina nodded then turned and left.

I could only hope that my assignment was as easy as Gina's. The thought of someone dining so early in the evening left me in disbelief. I knew I would be famished by the time I finally settled into bed if I ate this early.

Shirley scrutinized me with a piercing gaze, her expression critical and unyielding. It felt like an eternity as I stood there, second guessing whether I had accidentally worn my pants inside out. The absence of a tag or pockets left me to make an educated guess, and I hoped desperately that I hadn't messed up my wardrobe.

"I have to say, you look incredible for just having a baby. Is it a boy or a girl?" she finally said.

I hesitated, momentarily caught off guard forgetting I was supposed to have a newborn baby at home. The notion of parenthood was still foreign to me, as I had never experienced it myself and had limited exposure to children. The thought that people would ask about my nonexistent baby hadn't even crossed my mind. I must have paused for too long because I could see her eyebrow shoot up, questioning my silence.

"I'm sorry. When you mentioned the baby, it made me realize how much I missed her already. Her name's Georgia." I blurted out the first thought that came to my mind.

"That's sweet." Her smile returned. "Come, let me introduce you to the rest of the staff."

As we strolled down the dimly lit hallway, each step echoed on the polished floors as we neared the nurse's station at the center of the building.

"How long have you been nursing?" Shirley asked.

"About eight years," I replied, maintaining an air of confidence.

Inwardly, I hoped she wouldn't probe too deeply. My medical knowledge was largely shaped by the television show, Grey's Anatomy, which I had binge-watched just the night before. I silently prayed that this job wouldn't be as fraught with tension and drama as the world portrayed on screen.

We arrived at a small nurse's desk. A single computer was stationed at the center, flanked by three chairs, two of which were already occupied.

"This is Bridget and T.J.," she said, introducing the man and woman sitting behind the desk.

Bridget was in her mid-forties with red hair pulled back into a tidy ponytail. She wore neon lime green scrubs that were so bright they almost reflected the fluorescent lights. Wow, I thought. At that moment, I couldn't help but think my purple scrubs weren't looking so bad.

T.J. appeared to be around my age and was wearing olive green scrubs. His wavy brown hair framed a face marked by a distinctive feature. His imposing nose was the size of a dill pickle. It was bent to the left, most likely because it was broken sometime in the past.

"This is Sydney," Shirley introduced me.

"Nice to meet you," Bridget said. "Do you have any pictures of your baby?"

Not being particularly fond of children, I had

never truly grasped the extent of others' obsession with them. As I observed T.J. glancing impatiently at his watch, I couldn't help but wonder if only women possessed that innate ability to adore babies. My mind raced, as I went with the first excuse that popped into my head.

"I left my purse in the car."

"No problem, you can show them to us tomorrow," Bridgett said.

Great, I thought. Where on earth was I going to find a baby picture? Maybe I could steal one from the Internet.

Suddenly, ringing echoed from all three of their pockets. I watched as Bridget fished a phone from her front pocket, glancing at the screen before answering. Her expression shifted as she engaged in a brief conversation, then dropped the phone back into her pocket.

"Come on T.J., Mrs. Bennett needs help getting her husband in the shower." Both she and T.J. rose from their seats and made their way down the hallway.

"You all have a phone that rings when someone needs you?" I asked.

"Yes, all the phones will ring until one person answers. Don't worry. While you're getting oriented, you won't need to worry about the phones. You can assist one of the others for the next week or so," Shirley explained. "Now, let's go around the desk and I'll show you how the computer works."

As I rounded the desk, I caught a glimpse across the hall into the dining room. I spotted Gina leaning casually against a mop, deep in conversation with an elderly woman seated at one of the tables. The woman's face was animated, as she seemed to be talking about something, and I hoped that Gina was absorbing something valuable from their interaction.

Shirley informed me that the building was

exclusively comprised of single-bedroom apartments, each designed to offer residents a sense of independence. The residents typically only called them when they had a specific need. The computer contained a comprehensive list of their medications and health issues.

As I leaned closer to the screen, she began to guide me through how the software on the computer worked. For the next thirty minutes, we navigated through the charts. I was so bored that I found myself stifling yawns, nodding along while my mind drifted. I pictured myself on a beach drinking a margarita, served by a tanned, muscular waiter ready to cater to my every whim. Finally, the torture came to an end when the shrill ring of her phone cut through the air.

"Uh-huh. I'll be right down." Shirley rose from the desk. "Mr. Bennett is starting to get Alzheimer's and sometimes forgets where he is. He's trying to jump out of the second-floor window. If you'll excuse me for a moment. Go ahead and get familiar with the computer while I'm gone."

I quickly scuttled my chair closer to the computer as she hurried away. With a few clicks, I navigated away from the patient list and began to skim through the files, scanning for anything useful. My eyes fell upon a document labeled 'Employee Schedule.' I opened it eagerly and found that the schedule covered the entire year. I clicked the print button and made a copy of the schedule from the beginning of the year through this month. I gathered the printed copies, folded them, and placed them in my pocket.

As I continued to sift through the files, an old gray-haired man approached the desk. His skin hung loosely from his bones, and he had more wrinkles on his face than the shirt I crumpled up and tossed in the corner of my bedroom last night. He wore a burgundy terrycloth robe that looked worn and faded, hinting at its years of use. He just stood there, silently observing me. I rose from my chair and leaned slightly forward.

"May I help you?" I asked, praying that whatever he needed would be straightforward and not require a medical degree to resolve.

He whipped open his robe and stood there in all his glory, stark naked. I quickly realized what was worse than seeing an old person's butt. It was an old man's junk. His manhood hung limp, wrinkled and shriveled up to the size of a paper clip. A small paper clip.

I arched my eyebrow, a mixture of amusement and disgust playing across my face.

He glanced down at his minuscule appendage, an embarrassed flush creeping onto his cheeks. "It's cold in here," he mumbled, trying to justify himself.

"Obviously."

Hurriedly, he tightly closed his robe and scurried down the hallway.

After the nurses returned, Shirley excused herself and headed to the office. I continued talking with T.J. while Bridget talked on her cell phone.

"So, how long have you worked here?" I asked.

T.J. leaned back in his chair. "Over two years. It's not a bad job. There's a lot of downtime."

"Are the residents here a long time?"

"Depends on their health. Some only stay for a few months, others are here for years. Harry Thompson has been here over ten years now."

"Do the residents ever die?"

He shrugged nonchalantly, a hint of weariness in his voice. "It's something you get used to as a nurse. Patients passing away become part of the job. Sometimes, though, it's not just about death; there are times when patients can no longer care for themselves, and they need to transition to a nursing home. If Mr. Bennett's memory continues to fade, we'll have no choice but to transfer him to an Alzheimer's unit."

"What's the protocol when someone dies?"

"The family is notified, and then the morgue comes and picks them up. It's a straightforward process."

"Aren't the police notified?" I was surprised that more wasn't done in such situations.

T.J. shook his head and gave me a sharp look. "No, why would they be? Everyone here is old and dies eventually."

This would definitely be a place where it wouldn't be hard to commit a murder unnoticed. If every fatality could so easily be classified as natural, there would be no reason for an investigation to unfold.

T.J. yawned, his body arching as he stretched his arms above his head.

"Has there been any recent deaths?" I asked.

He lowered his arms and locked eyes with me. I could feel his gaze piercing through my facade. "You seem really interested in death," he noted, a hint of suspicion lingering in his tone.

"I have always found death the saddest part of the job." If I didn't change the topic soon, I knew he would grow suspicious. "So, what does T.J. stand for?"

"Total jerk," Bridget chimed in with a smirk.

"Ha, ha," T.J. responded. "It stands for Tyler Jackson. My last name is Rotz." He rose from his chair and stretched. "Now if you've finished the interrogation, I'm going to take a walk and stretch my legs."

"Don't mind him. He isn't very social. So, tell me about your baby girl."

Just then, a loud vroom filled the air. I glanced up to see Gina vacuuming the carpet in front of the desk. It was too loud to continue the conversation, and I was grateful for the interruption.

The rest of the evening was uneventful. I engaged the nurses in light-hearted discussions about the residents and their daily routines, carefully avoiding any sensitive subjects like the heavy burden of resident deaths or worse, babies. Every so often, one of the nurses would rise to assist a resident, administering medications or helping them prepare for bed, but for the most part, they remained at the desk. After the residents settled down for the evening, I was sent home. I met Gina in the car since she walked out about half an hour before me.

After our surveillance job, Gina rushed home, eager to prepare for her date. On any other day, her driving felt like a thrill ride at an amusement park, fast and chaotic. I often wanted to throw my hands up and shout, "Whee!" as we zipped around corners. But when she was in a hurry, the experience transformed into something downright terrifying. I gripped the overhead bar tightly as we careened around a bend, the tires squealing and the car clipping the curb with a jolt.

"Don't you think you should slow down?" I asked, my heart racing.

She shot me an amused glance. "I've seen how you drive, so you have no room to talk."

"I at least stay between the lines."

"That's not fair. Your motorcycle is smaller than my car."

As we careened into the driveway, the tires squealed against the asphalt. The moment the engine's roar faded, Gina sprang from her seat, leaping out of the car. She dashed toward the house like a whirlwind. I spotted Krista's SUV pulling in behind the Mustang.

"What are you doing here?" I asked as she emerged from the car.

"I came to help Gina get ready for her date."

I couldn't help but smirk. "You would be a better choice than me," I admitted, knowing full well that Krista's fashion sense far surpassed mine.

Gina hadn't asked me to help her get ready for a

good reason. I didn't keep up with the latest trends. If I was going on a date, I would wear what was comfortable and practical. That would certainly not include a dress, especially since I didn't even own one. And if I couldn't wear my combat boots, I wouldn't go at all.

I waited downstairs while Gina got primped and polished for her date. The minutes ticked by, and after what felt like an eternity, Krista and Gina emerged from upstairs.

Her black hair was curled and wavy. Her violet dress clung to her figure, and her striking purple eyeliner matched it.

"You look great." Maybe a little vampire-like, but who was I to judge?

"Thanks," she beamed.

"Is he coming to pick you up?" I asked.

They both looked at me as if I had just spoken in an alien language.

"What?"

"I'm meeting him at the restaurant. When you meet someone online, it's a rule of thumb not to reveal your home address. That's just asking to become a victim of a stalker."

"Or serial killer," Krista added. "Don't you ever date?"

"Other soldiers or someone where I live. The world of online dating is completely foreign to me."

"Surely they have online dating in Europe?" Krista asked.

I shrugged. To be honest, I had no idea because I'd never bothered to check. When you work intelligence, maintaining a low profile is essential, and cultivating minimal social media presence is part of the strategy. The last thing an undercover agent needed was for their identity to be plastered all over the Internet for anyone to see.

That happened to my friend Arnold. He had a big takedown, and a bystander caught the whole thing on their phone. The footage quickly found its way onto YouTube, and just like that, Arnold's covert life was exposed. Because of the incident, Arnold now had a desk job. As for me, I've made a conscious choice to stay off any social media platforms. I don't use Facebook, Twitter, or any other platform. As far as I knew, there were no photographs of me floating around the digital clouds of the Internet, and I intended to keep it that way.

"So, tell us about the guy you're meeting tonight. You know, in case he is a serial killer and you don't make it home," I joked.

Gina shot me a daggered glare. "His name is Ted. We're meeting at Appalachia."

"Fancy," I remarked. Appalachia was the nicest restaurant in Gettysburg. Although it wouldn't earn a Michelin star in New York City, Appalachia was known for its impeccable fusion of German and Irish cuisine.

After Gina left, Krista plopped down on the couch next to me. "I wanted to let you know that the approval to exhume Teresa's mother came through. They're going to do it first thing in the morning."

"Why so early?"

"They wanted to do it before the cemetery opened to the public."

That made sense. Most people wouldn't enjoy the unsettling sight of a coffin being unearthed from the ground.

"Mind if I stick around?" Krista asked. "I want to see how her date goes."

"Let me make some popcorn."

While I made the popcorn, Krista skimmed through the television channels, her voice floating to me as she called out movie options. I chose the movie theater popcorn with extra butter. Eating popcorn without a generous dose of butter was a sin. Krista wanted to watch a rom-com, and I wanted to watch something a little more edgy, like Freddie Krueger. We eventually compromised on 'Weekend at Bernie's.'

"This is the stupidest movie," Krista complained, popping a kernel of popcorn in her mouth. "Who steals a dead body and pretends it's alive?"

"That's what makes it funny."

As we sat there, the dim light from the TV flicking, Gina emerged from the kitchen. I grabbed the remote control and hit the pause button, freezing the scene on the screen.

"You're home early," I said.

"This can't be good. Was the date that bad?" Krista inquired.

"Actually, he was a nice guy. As I stepped into the restaurant, I spotted him already sitting at a table. When he saw me, he jumped up and met me at the door. He even pulled my chair out for me."

"Are guys allowed to do that anymore?" I asked.

Krista shrugged. "Was he boring?"

"No, he works as a press secretary out of Frederick. He told hilarious stories about politicians behaving badly." She abruptly tossed her purse onto the table, the thud echoing in the quiet room. Krista and I exchanged glances. Gina flopped down into the recliner.

"So, as we ordered drinks, I notice this woman sitting at the table next to ours," Gina continued. "She was unashamedly leaning in, clearly eavesdropping on our conversation. Ted excused himself to use the restroom, and that's when the woman's gaze homed in on me as if I were sprouting antennae right out of my head. When Ted returned, I asked him if he knew the woman."

"And?" Krista leaned forward, perched on the edge of her seat, her eyes wide with anticipation.

"It was his mother," Gina revealed.

"No," Krista gasped, covering her mouth with her hand.

"You're making this up," I said.

Gina shook her head, her expression serious. "He told me he hoped I wouldn't be upset that he brought her along because she was his best friend."

I didn't even know how to process that information. "What did you do?"

"I excused myself to the restroom."

"Then what?" Krista asked.

"That's it," she said with a smirk. "I walked straight past the restrooms and out the front door."

I couldn't help myself. Laughter bubbled up inside me, erupting until my chest ached. Gina and Krista joined in the laughter. Krista's laughter turned into a contagious giggle fit, and as she leaned over, she unexpectedly lost her balance and tumbled off the couch, which only escalated our hilarity. As we finally calmed down, I could already feel the familiar throb in my ribs.

"If that's what online dating is like you can count me out," I said, still giggling.

"I'm happy I'm married," Krista said.

Gina crossed her arms and huffed in an attempt to look mad, but a chuckle escaped her lips. "I'm glad the two of you are getting such kicks from the worst date of my life."

"It's not that big a deal," Krista said.

"Easy for you to say. You've been with Sean since your first year of college."

Krista shrugged. "I'm sure Sydney has had her fair share of bad dating experiences."

My laughter faded as I felt a familiar weight settle over me, and my expression turned to a blank slate. Memories I tried so hard to bury resurfaced, especially thoughts of one particular person.

Gina, sensing my change in mood, leaned

forward and plucked the remote from my hand.

"Let's finish the movie," she said, swiftly changing the conversation. She understood the complexities of my past with Jason, but she also knew I didn't want to talk about it. Some things, after all, were meant to be left buried in the depths of memory, untouched and undisturbed.

CHAPTER 7

I dragged myself out of bed at the crack of dawn the next morning. The early morning light filtered through the curtains, casting soft shadows on the floor. As I trudged down the stairs, the familiar scent of brewing coffee wafted up from the kitchen, urging me forward. Stepping into the room, I found Gina slumped at the table, her head resting unceremoniously on her hands, eyes shut tight as if trying to ward off the world.

"You awake?"

"Barely," she groaned. "Who gets up at this ungodly hour?"

The coffee pot was already gurgling as a slow, steady stream of dark liquid poured into the pot.

"Can you get the sugar out of the pantry for me? I'm too tired to get up and need the extra carbs this morning to get moving."

Yesterday, while in the pantry, I spotted the sugar bag on the second shelf inside the door. I was too tired to turn the light in the pantry on and besides, at this time of the morning my eyes wouldn't take the bright light. The soft glow from the kitchen casted just enough illumination to reveal the sugar. I had just touched the bag when a pain erupted in my head- sharp and intense, as if someone had driven a nail straight into my skull. I felt the pain a second time and saw fireworks behind my eyelids.

Instinctively, I covered my head with my hand, ducking down, hoping to shield myself from whatever chaos awaited me. I cautiously looked up, and my eyes fell upon Cagney and Lacey, who were perched on the top shelf. Their beady eyes were fixed on me, offering a judgmental glare. Lacey chose that exact moment to relieve herself, and before I could react, a plop of chicken poop landed squarely on my forehead. I wrinkled my brow in disgust and wiped it off, flinging it on the pantry floor. I quickly retreated from the pantry before any more mishaps befell me.

"Why are the chickens in the pantry?" I asked as I stormed over to the sink to get a rag and soap to wash my face.

"They needed someplace to stay," Gina responded, not even opening her eyes, seemingly unfazed by the chaos.

"What about the garage?"

"I park the Mustang in there. I don't want them to scratch the paint."

Gina's pride and joy was her vintage Mustang from the early seventies. It was a vibrant yellow that reminded me of Tweety Bird.

"So, you thought the pantry was the best place for them?" I sometimes questioned Gina's logic.

Gina sat up and stretched. "I could have put them in your room instead."

The pantry it was, I thought resignedly.

* * * *

We arrived at the cemetery shortly before seven. Walter, Krista, and Sean were already there, their faces solemn as they watched an excavator remove dirt from the grave. We were walking towards the graveside when

Sheriff Earl and another man ambled towards us from the opposite direction. I tried not to wince when I saw the other man, John Martin.

John was the mortician at the local funeral home. Just last month, my mother thought it was a good idea to invite him over for dinner, in an attempt to set me up on a date. I wasn't happy about it, to begin with, but the revelation that he had four little kids concreted it. I had slipped away from the table just before dessert and snuck out of the house.

The sheriff looked at me with a dislike that was mutual.

"What are you doing here?" he spat, his voice low and threatening. "I warned you to stay out of my investigation or else."

"Technically," I couldn't help but point out, "you told us to avoid interfering with the body under the shed. This isn't the same situation at all."

"Do you want to go to jail?" he growled through clenched teeth. "I'm ordering you to leave now or-"

"Sydney and Gina are here with us in an official capacity," Walter interjected firmly.

The sheriff's eyes narrowed, and I had to bite my tongue to keep from sticking it out at him. He stalked away to the other side of the grave, the tension in the air palpable.

"Wow," John said. "I don't think the sheriff likes you much."

"I got that feeling too," I replied, glancing towards the sheriff's retreating form.

"Speaking of feelings, have you been feeling better since last I saw you?"

God only knows what excuse my mother had concocted for my abrupt departure at our last meeting. Before I could respond, a loud diesel truck rumbled to a stop beside the grave. It was towing a bright red platform with an imposing lift arm positioned in the center. At the ends of the forks, two thick straps dangled, resembling oversized rubber bands that I figured stretch beneath the casket to lift it out.

Half a dozen men materialized out of nowhere and hopped into the open grave. The arm descended into the pit with the men. After several minutes and a few colorful curse words ascending from the hole, the engine on the platform roared to life. The arm slowly began to lift the silver casket from the ground. Aside from the dirt clinging to it, the casket appeared almost pristine. The men jumped out of the hole and pushed the arm around. With a thud, they lowered the casket into the bed of the diesel truck and the show was over.

As they covered the casket and secured it with heavy straps, a beige Lincoln Town car glided to a stop beside the truck.

The door swung open to reveal a man, his attire strikingly formal for the sweltering June heat. Gina had mentioned that this man was the local coroner.

Walter walked toward the idling car. He extended his hand in a gesture of greeting, but the coroner merely glanced at it, dismissing the gesture as he began to speak. You could sense the tension in the air as the coroner's hands clenched into tight fists, his voice rising enough to cut through the low rumble of the truck's engine, yet it was still too muffled to make out the words.

"Wonder what's got Ben so riled up?" Gina said.

"You never did tell me the coroners name."

"It's Benjamin Scott," Gina replied.

"He moved to town and took over after Charlie disappeared," Krista said.

"Where did he come from?"

"Some big city like Pittsburgh or New York."

"Wonder what made him want to move here?"

Krista shrugged.

72

Ben turned away, returned to the car, and slammed the door. He accelerated away, flinging gravel up behind him as he went.

Earl sauntered over and addressed Sean. "I'll see you at Rita's for lunch." He inclined his head towards Walter, then turned on his heels and strode away, choosing to ignore both Gina and me.

"Guess we're off his Christmas card list," I whispered to Gina, who preceded to stick her tongue out at his retreating figure.

"What's wrong with Ben?" Gina asked Walter when he returned to the group.

Walter sighed. "He's mad about the plans for Evaline's body."

"What happens to the body now?" I asked.

Walter leaned back on his heels, a contemplative look crossing his face. "An old friend of mine from college works as a forensic coroner in Boston. He specializes in examining bodies that have... well, let's just say they've had quite a bit of time to settle in."

"You mean like when they find a body in the woods that's been decomposing for years?" I asked.

Krista's face scrunched in distaste. "Eeew, that's disgusting."

"Yes, that is the blunt way of putting it." Walter adjusted his tie. "The casket will remain at the funeral home tonight and will be transferred to Boston in the morning."

"My funeral home has made all the arrangements for the transfer," John said proudly.

Walter continued, "Ben was eager to conduct the autopsy himself, but I insisted that a skilled specialist handle this case."

Sean's voice cut through the conversation. "Gina, I need to talk to you briefly before you leave."

"Come by and see me some time," John said as

he strolled back to the line of cars alongside Walter.

Meanwhile, Gina, Krista, and I stayed behind with Sean, who seemed slightly more serious than usual.

"I only need to speak with Gina," Sean stated.

"Oh, come on, she's going to spill the beans about your conversation as soon as you walk away," Krista pointed out.

The corners of Sean's mouth lifted in a reluctant smile. He knew he could never deny anything his wife suggested.

"Gina," he began, "how well did you know the couple who owned the house before you?"

"That really depends on who was beneath the coop." Gina responded.

He shook his head.

Krista crossed her arms, a hint of frustration etched on her face. "This isn't a bustling city. News like this has a way of leaking out, sooner or later."

"Sheriff Henderson has been biting everyone's head off since he returned. He had the night shift guy on his hands and knees scrubbing the floor for wishing him a good day. Can you imagine what he would do to me if he found out I told you?"

Gina's lower lip jutted out as she gave him her pleading puppy dog eyes.

He exhaled deeply, running a hand through his hair. "Blake is currently at Mrs. Winchester's apartment, conducting an interview with her. Perhaps you could drop by and pay her a visit later today."

Krista planted a soft peck on his cheek.

"Where is she living now?" I asked.

"She has an apartment at Meadow Springs," Sean replied, glancing at his watch. "I have to get back to the station." He leaned in for a quick kiss with Krista before turning to leave.

We waited for the sound of Sean's car to fade into

the distance before we could finally speak openly.

"We need to talk to Mini now," Gina said.

"I have to get back to work," Krista interjected.

"I need to stop by the house to put something together first," I said. "Blake should be done with Mini by then. Let's meet for lunch at the diner to discuss what we find."

"That sounds great," Krista said. "Besides, I still need to find out what happened last night."

"It's settled. We will meet around noon," Gina confirmed.

As we returned to the house, I made my way into the kitchen while Gina disappeared into her office.

Just as I slid my concoction into the freezer and gently closed the door, an ear-splitting crash erupted from somewhere within the house, reverberating through the walls and shaking the foundation beneath my feet. It felt as though a tornado had collided with an earthquake.

In a flurry of feathers and noise, the chickens erupted from the pantry, their frantic squawking and flapping wings creating a raucous scene as they dashed toward the back door. I swiftly pushed the back door open before racing into the living room as I tried to grasp what had just happened. The study door stood open, and as I peered inside, disbelief washed over me.

There was a car in the study. Half of a sleek white sedan jutted awkwardly through a gaping hole in the wall, its crumpled front end crammed into the room.

"Help!" I heard Gina's panicked voice from behind the door. The room was filled with dust, and debris was still falling from the ceiling. I edged into the room, wading through the remnants of shattered plaster and scattered papers. In the mist of the wreckage sat Gina, her expression a mix of fear and disbelief. She was trapped in her chair against the back wall, the sturdy desk pinning her in place.

"You okay?" I asked.

"Yeah. It's a good thing this chair has wheels or I might have been flattened like a pancake. Help me out."

I peered through the gaping hole in the wall to see the driver's side door open and Beatrix stumbling out.

"Who in their right mind puts a house right in the middle of a road?" she exclaimed. She slammed the driver's door, sending shards of glass cascading down like rain onto the car's already cracked windshield.

I shook my head in disbelief. Quickly, I pulled the desk away from Gina, creating an opening for her to escape.

"What have you done?" I heard Jean's frantic voice from the other side of the wall.

An unmarked black police car pulled into the driveway. Blake leaped out of the vehicle; urgency written all over his face.

"Is everyone okay?" he called out.

"Yes," I replied as I skirted around the car and came outside to assess the damage. The vehicle was positioned at an awkward angle, suggesting that Beatrix had carelessly darted out of her driveway, crossed the road in a reckless hurry, jumped the curb, and crashed spectacularly through the house's picture window.

Beside me, Gina emerged from the shadows, her face pale and eyes wide with shock. "I'm not alright," she exclaimed. "There is a car. IN MY HOUSE!"

"I'm so sorry." Jean apologized and then turned toward her mother. "What were you thinking? You aren't allowed to drive."

"I have to get to work."

It was a scary thought to think that Beatrix ever drove. The mere thought of her driving was enough to make my skin crawl.

"You haven't worked in thirty years," Jean shot back, frustration etched on her face.

Just then, the wail of sirens pierced the air as an ambulance pulled up behind Blake's car. Despite Beatrix's vehement protests, the paramedics carefully loaded her onto a stretcher and prepared to take her to the hospital for a check-up. Beatrix cursed loudly, her voice a relentless stream of expletives directed at her captors. I couldn't help but feel sorry for the crew who had to endure her wrath the whole way to the hospital.

The fire marshal arrived and, after a careful inspection of the house, concluded that it was still livable. He noted that the car had miraculously missed all the support beams, ensuring the structure remained sound despite the damage.

Several neighbors had gathered on the sidewalk, their smartphones capturing the moment, ready to share the spectacle on social media within minutes.

Finally, Willy pulled up in his tow truck to remove the car from the house. He promised Gina that he and his cousin would secure the front of the house with boards until proper repairs could be arranged.

After the excitement, we made our way to Meadow Springs to talk to Mini. As we stepped through the sliding glass doors, I was surprised to spot Shirley near the front desk.

"What are you doing here this early? Your shift doesn't start until later," Shirley said.

"We came to visit an old friend of mine," Gina said. "Mini Winchester."

"She's certainly popular today. You'll find her upstairs in apartment forty-two."

We took the elevator upstairs and walked down the corridor, following the numbers to forty-two. I raised my hand and knocked gently on the door.

"Hold your horses," came a voice from within. "Can't an old woman get any rest?"

The door opened, and I was taken aback by the

sight before me. I was expecting an old shrunken dinosaur like Beatrix, but this woman seemed decades younger than the metazoic era old biddies across the street. Her platinum white hair was cut into a bob that framed her face. Instead of a flowered old lady's dress, she wore a cream-colored blouse and tan slacks.

"I know you," she said as she peered at Gina over the rim of her retro turquoise glasses. "You bought my house. I know why you are here. Come in."

She opened the door wider and waved us in, revealing a cozy apartment. We entered the small kitchen, which opened into the living room. She ushered us in, and we sat on the couch.

"This is my niece, Sydney," Gina introduced.

"Minerva, but Mini to my friends. Can I offer you something to drink?" she asked.

We politely declined.

She wasted no time getting to the heart of the matter. "I assume you're here because the police found Charlie under the chicken coop."

I appreciated her directness.

"So, they told you?" Gina asked.

She gave a single nod. "They used his dental records to confirm it. If I remember you are a PI, so you probably have some questions."

Gina and I looked at each other unsure how to ask the next question.

Mini read our hesitation. "Go ahead and ask. I have nothing to hide. To answer your thoughts, no, I didn't kill him, and no, I don't know how he ended up under the coop. I truly believed he left with one of the many bimbos he cheated on me with."

A tea kettle on the stove let out a piercing whistle. Mini rose from her chair, her bare feet making no noise as she moved to pour herself a cup of steaming tea.

"I honestly didn't miss him once he was gone. I

liked my chickens far more than him." Her eyes brightened with fondness. After a brief pause, she asked, "How are Cagney and Lacey doing?"

"Energetic as ever," Gina said, eliciting a smile from Mini.

"When did you notice Charlie was missing?" Gina asked.

"It was the night before the concrete was poured for the shed. I remember because that night, I thought to myself, if I had known he was going to leave, I wouldn't have had the cement put in. The shed had been there for years, but he wanted a concrete floor so he could turn it into a workshop. Several days before, the construction company came in and lifted the shed up on blocks and got the ground ready to pour the cement."

"Can you run us through the events of the day the floor was poured?" I asked.

"Charlie was already gone that morning when I got up. That night, Charlie didn't come home. The next morning, when I woke up and realized he wasn't back yet, I knew something was wrong, so I called the police. Charlie's car had vanished along with him, and I noticed a sizable amount of money missing from our checking account. Everyone assumed he had left town."

"Was it normal for him to leave before you woke up in the morning?" Gina inquired.

"Absolutely," she blew on her hot tea and took a tentative sip. "He often received calls at all hours, his duties as a coroner required him to respond to all unexpected deaths, whether they occurred in a car accident or at someone's home."

"Did he have any enemies?" Gina asked.

"Just the husbands of the women he was sleeping with," she said with a hint of bitterness. "You're probably wondering why I chose to stay with him. Charlie may have been a crappy husband, but he provided for his family. Back in my day, options for a woman leaving her husband were incredibly limited. I didn't have an education beyond high school to fall back on. If I had left him, I likely would have been forced to live on the streets with no clear path for supporting my children. So, I decided to tolerate his indiscretions and carried on with my life as best as I could. The silver lining was that he was never at home. He was either at work, spending time with one of his women, or at the gym."

"He spent a lot of time in the gym?"

"Oh yes. He was there almost every day. Sometimes for hours at a time."

"Do you know the names of any of the women he was cheating with?"

She flashed us a sly smile. "Sorry, he didn't divulge that information to me."

"Do you recall the name of the company that handled the work on the shed?"

"It was JK Construction."

I had no further questions lingering in my mind, so I stood to leave. Gina followed suit.

"Thank you for your time," I said.

She waved her hand dismissively. "Just let me know if I can help in any way."

"Could you do me a favor and keep our meeting under wraps? The sheriff doesn't want us getting involved in his case."

She frowned. "The sheriff is a jackass. Don't worry, I never saw you."

As we strode across the parking lot, I cast a glance at Gina.

"How are we supposed to talk to the construction company without the sheriff finding out?" I asked.

"Don't worry. I have an idea," came her reply.

CHAPTER 8

When we called JK Construction, the secretary informed us the crew was remodeling a building in town. When we arrived at the site, three workers in yellow hard hats carefully carried a massive piece of glass toward the structure. A separate man wearing an orange hard hat stood out as he barked orders at his team. We nudged our way past the bright yellow caution tape, approaching him.

"Excuse me," Gina said.

His expression darkened, clearly irritated that we had interrupted his workflow. "What do you want?"

"We're searching for Jacob."

"You've found him," Jacob replied, his gaze locked onto the trio of workers outside who were carefully maneuvering the large pane of glass into the expansive opening at the front of the store. A fourth worker appeared inside, struggling to stabilize the heavy glass.

"Your secretary mentioned we could find you here. I need some repairs done to my house."

"Are you looking for a new roof? New siding?"

"Actually, there's a car parked in my study."

That caught his attention, and his gaze finally shifted to Gina. "There's a car inside your house?" he asked with a mix of disbelief and curiosity.

Gina pulled up a picture on her phone and showed it to him.

He leaned in, squinting against the bright sun, trying to make out the details in the image. "Huh, there's a car in your house," he said, stating the obvious. He studied the picture. "I know this house."

Gina nodded. "The previous owner, Mini, told me you were the best, and I should have you fix the house."

"Ah yes, the dead guy under the shed." He turned his gaze back toward the building. "Juan, make sure to screw those brackets in tightly to secure it." Turning his attention back to Gina, he continued, "I can arrange for a couple of guys to come over next week to begin the work. In the meantime, do you need it boarded up?"

"No, a friend is taking care of that for me right now."

He nodded. "It's a shame about them finding Charlie under the shed."

"Mini mentioned that your company poured the cement." Gina, placing her hand dramatically on her chest, feigned surprise as if the thought just came to her. "Do you think Charlie was under there before the cement was laid?"

His cheeks flushed a deep crimson, a rush of anger flooding his face. "That bumbling Sheriff Henderson seemed convinced it was our fault," he snapped.

"He can be an idiot," I offered, intentionally stoking the flames.

"I can think of a better word. He tried to blame me for it, claiming I was responsible for Charlie's death, that I had buried him beneath the concrete to conceal the body." He shook his head in disbelief. "I set him straight. Charlie paid me upfront for the work, and I held no grudge against him. There was never any reason for me to want him dead."

"What do you think happened?" I pressed.

"I don't know." His gaze shifted back to the crew,

where a buzzing noise began as they screwed a cord around the window frame. "It's like I told the cops. We raised the shed and prepped the ground on Friday. By Monday, we were pouring the cement. But during the weekend, I have no idea what happened."

"You remember all that?" Gina asked.

He shook his head. "No, it's on the old work order I pulled out and showed the sheriff."

"Thanks for your help." Gina called out as the drilling stopped. She reached into her pocket and handed Jacob a business card. With a nod of appreciation, we turned and made our way back to the car.

Unfortunately, as we strolled past the construction crew, Gina suddenly stumbled when her foot caught on a discarded drill. Her arms flailed wildly as she tried desperately to regain her balance. Despite her efforts, she lost her footing and flew forward, hurtling toward the sidewalk. Just ahead, a board was perched atop an overturned bucket. To break her fall, Gina thrust her hands forward, inadvertently striking the top corner of the board. In an instant, the opposite end of the board shot upwards, launching a hammer that had been resting there. The tool soared through the air like a disoriented pigeon.

The hammer struck the glass pane dead center with a sharp crack, sending it shattering into a thousand shards, littering the sidewalk below. The spectacle captured the attention of all four construction workers, who turned toward Gina, their mouths agape in disbelief.

The sound of the glass breaking resonated through the air like a bomb exploding, snapping everyone's attention on the street. Everything became still and silent.

From her shop across the street, Genesis emerged, intrigued by the commotion. I gave her a warm smile and waved. She surveyed the scattering of glass covering the pavement, her eyes shifting to Gina, who was propping herself up on her knees. Genesis smiled softly, shaking her head in amusement, before retreating into her shop.

I extended my hand to Gina, gently pulling her up from the ground. As we stood, we glanced back at the foreman, whose thick brows were knitted tightly together and whose face had turned such a shade of red that I thought his head would pop.

"Whenever you make it to the house works for me," Gina remarked as we hightailed it out of there.

* * * *

We swung by the house so I could retrieve my frozen treats. Willy and his cousin were already hard at work, hammering large sheets of plywood against the front of the house. Gina paused for a brief chat with them, her voice light and cheerful, while I darted inside, eager to see my creation.

As I opened the freezer, a rush of frigid air enveloped me, causing my sunglasses to fog up and a chill to dance across my nose. I leaned in, squinting through the mist, and felt a surge of excitement wash over me as I spotted my creation, which was perfectly set. If everything went according to plan, this would be epic. I dumped them into a thermos and dashed back outside.

Krista was already settled into the booth at the far end of the diner when we walked in. I slid in beside her to keep an eye on the entrance. Gina took the seat across from us.

As soon as we sat down, Krista said, "You could have called me and told me you weren't hurt."

"You heard about that already?" You would think in a town as small as Gettysburg, the rumor mill would churn a little more slowly.

She pulled out her phone and displayed a video on the screen. It captured the scene outside Gina's house, where Willy was maneuvering his tow truck to extract a car from the middle of the house. "I received three Instagram posts and one TikTok video in less than an hour," she remarked a hint of disbelief in her voice.

I chuckled to myself. So much for slow-moving news in a small town.

"Start by telling me about your undercover mission at Meadow Springs last night," Krista said, her eyes scanning the menu as she pondered her choice.

Rita's Diner had been a staple in our town long before I took my first breath. The menu remained unchanged throughout the years. The worn laminate covering the menu had faded to a light yellow hue, with the edges curling up. Given how frequently Krista had dined here over the years, you'd think the items would be etched in her memory by now. I hadn't lived here for over ten years, and I pretty much had it down pat.

"Well..." Gina began, her voice trailing off as a shadow fell over the table.

We glanced up to find Dominic standing over us. He was dressed in an electric blue polo shirt and was carrying a vibrant purple backpack. The bag was adorned with pink and purple rhinestones that sparkled in the light.

"Nice purse," I teased with a grin.

"It's my computer bag, thank you very much. My niece thought it was imperative to bedazzle it for me."

I wasn't entirely sure what 'bedazzled' meant, but I hoped it had something to do with the glistening gemstones on it.

"Can I join you, lovely ladies?" He flopped down next to Gina, slipping his bag in between them.

The three of us exchanged uneasy glances. How were we supposed to continue our serious discussion about business with this unexpected addition at our table?

Dominic must have sensed our predicament because he leaned in slightly, his gaze shifting between us. "So, are we going to discuss the dead body under the coop, or shall we talk about the grave desecration you all participated in this morning?"

Kirsta's jaw dropped, her eyes wide with surprise. "How did you know about the graveyard?"

"Devna told me about it when I was shopping for a new pair of Gucci's this morning." He extended his leg into the aisle, lifting his foot to showcase his sleek black leather sneakers.

If Devna was aware of the body's removal from the cemetery, word must have spread like wildfire through the town. Devna owned Sundara, a chic, upscale clothing store. She was notorious for being the town gossip. She seemed to have a talent for collecting secrets, often learning about events before they even unfolded.

"Nice sneakers," I remarked. Of course, I couldn't tell the difference between a pair of Gucci shoes from twenty-dollar department store shoes.

"What makes you think we were planning to discuss either one of those events?"

"Please..." he exclaimed, his hand slicing through the air with dramatic flair. "It's not every day you steal a body from a grave or discover a skeleton lurking in your backyard. Besides," he looked me in the eyes, "I've known you my whole life. There's no way you are going to let this go without sticking your nose in it. Please let me know what's going on," he begged.

As children, Dominic and I shared everything—our secrets, our dreams, our adventures, creating a bond that made it difficult for me to keep him in the dark now. I turned to Krista and Gina, my expression pleading, silently asking for their support. They exchanged knowing smiles and nodded in agreement, granting me the unspoken permission to bring Dominic in.

"You have to keep everything you hear to yourself," I warned.

He clamped his mouth shut, then theatrically drew his hand in front of his lips as though he were turning a key to lock them. He then tossed the imaginary key over his shoulder. "Now, tell me about the body snatching first. It sounds absolutely fascinating."

"Let me start at the beginning." I detailed the mysterious deaths at the apartment complex, then relayed information about our escapade there last night. I finished the story with the morning cemetery event.

At that moment, the waitress approached our table, ready to take our drink orders. As I ordered an iced tea, I noticed her glance at the thermos perched beside my plate, but she didn't comment. Gina, seemingly shaken from her lousy date the night before, ordered chicken fingers, chips, and a chocolate milkshake. It was clear she had decided to forgo her diet.

"I retrieved the employee schedule and printed it from the main computer at the nurse's desk. The document spanned the past six months and included valuable information about the current residents. However, I was unable to locate any files regarding past residents."

"They're probably not stored on the main computer," Krista said. "There's no reason for the staff to need that information. But by law, all medical facilities are required to retain old records for a minimum of ten years. They might be archived in a separate office on a different computer."

The conversation paused as the waitress returned with our drinks.

"I agree," Dominic said. "If you give me the list of employees, I can conduct a background check on each one of them. This might reveal if there's anything suspicious in their history or any current involvement in shady activities."

"You don't mind?" I asked. Since Dominic was a

tech genius, I knew if there was any dirt to be dug up on the Internet, he would find it. He'd probably be able to find a math test that one of them failed in the eighth grade.

"Of course not," he replied with a casual wave of his hand. "Honestly, I've been bored since I retired."

A couple of months ago he struck gold by selling a computer application for a butt load of money. After that, he left his position at a prominent tech company. Now, I imagined him as a digital vigilante, probably spending his days and nights hacking away at challenges on his own terms.

Gina rummaged through her purse before finally retrieving the employee list and schedule. She handed the documents to Dominic, who slipped them into the front pocket of his bag.

"Why do you want a list of dead residents? That's creepy," Dominic asked.

"I'm hoping the list will include the dates and times of their deaths," I replied.

Domonic's head bobbed in understanding. "Ah, I see. It'll allow you to cross-reference the deaths with the work schedules of specific employees."

"Exactly," I affirmed. "If we can uncover the cause of death for each individual, we might just identify a pattern."

"If you can get me that list, I'll whip up a spreadsheet and analyze the data you need," Dominic said. "I could even hack the local hospital's database to check if the causes of death align with their existing health issues."

Just then, the waitress glided up to our table, balancing plates of steaming food while expertly refilling our drinks.

"Do you have any idea where the list of dead residents could be?" Krista asked after the waitress left.

I paused, taking a bite of my juicy turkey on rye

sandwich while contemplating the question. "It's likely tucked away in the head nurse's office," I replied, swallowing. "The problem is the head nurse spent most of her shift there last night, so we'd have to be careful."

With a mischievous glint in her eye, Gina crunched down on a potato chip. "I can create a distraction for you while you grab the information."

"Minor distraction," I suggested.

Gina raised her hand, her fingers held apart slightly as if to emphasize her point. "Very small."

I nodded.

"What if the computer's locked or I struggle to find the file?"

Dominic pushed his plate aside, the sound of it scraping against the table breaking the conversation's flow. He thudded his computer case down in front of him with a thump. With deliberate movements, he unzipped a small pocket on the bag and pulled out a thumb drive, its sleek surface gleaming under the overhead lights.

"Here," he said, extending the drive toward me. "Take this with you. Just slip it into the computer."

"It's just a thumb drive," I said skeptically. "What could it possibly do?"

A devilish smile flickered across Dominic's face. "No, it's a rubber ducky."

I raised an eyebrow, glancing down at the small green object cradled in my palm. "But it's not even yellow," I pointed out, and it didn't resemble any duck I had ever seen.

Dominic rolled his eyes at my lack of tech knowledge. "It's called a rubber ducky because of what it does," he explained.

Curiosity piqued, Gina leaned in closer, her eyes narrowing with interest. "What does it do?"

"When you slip it into the computer, it will immediately start downloading all the files, bypassing the most secure password protections. I have engineered this tool to strip the information from any computer in less than two minutes."

Krista's voice broke through, laced with apprehension. "Is it legal?" she asked, her brow knitting together in concern. At this juncture in her internship, with the end looming just around the corner, the ramifications of our actions weighed heavily on her mind. The fear of being disbarred before she could even step into her career as a lawyer concerned her.

We all exchanged glances.

She threw up her hands in exasperation. "Well, someone has to ask."

"Technically no," Dominic said.

When has that ever stopped us? I thought.

"But the beauty of this device," he continued, excitement sparkling in his eyes, "is that the computer reads it like keystrokes, almost as if a person is typing them out. Because of this, it doesn't trigger any antivirus alerts and leaves no trace behind. It's completely untraceable."

Dominic truly was a genius. I slipped the drive into my pocket and shared the details of our conversation with Mini Winchester.

"Bodyworks is the only gym in town," Krista declared.

"After lunch, we should swing by and see if they remember Charlie," Gina responded. "Maybe someone there can recall if he regularly hung out with anyone."

"I'm a member there. I can go with you," Dominic interjected.

We all sat quietly for a bit while we finished our meals. As I popped the last bite of my sandwich into my mouth, I couldn't shake the haunting image of Teresa's mother, whom we had pulled from the cold earth just that morning. If there was anything unusual about her death, how would we ever uncover the truth? It could take weeks or months before the pathologist in Boston returned any answers to Walter regarding the tests he would perform.

"I want to see Evaline's body tonight," I heard myself say. "Before it's transferred to Boston tomorrow."

Krista's fork halted midair, frozen in astonishment. Her eyes widened, a mixture of shock and horror playing across her face as she processed my words.

"Say what?" Dominic uttered, his voice cracking.

Gina's lips spread into a smile like a happy dog who has just caught a stick. This is one of the qualities I like most about Gina. No matter the absurdity of the proposition, she was always game. Want to infiltrate a secure Iranian military base and try to extract an American GI? Absolutely. Want to break into a funeral home in the dead of the night and get a glimpse of a corpse? Why not.

"What do you expect to find?" Krista finally asked after the shock of my suggestion wore off.

I shrugged. "Maybe nothing, but if something is lurking in the shadows, I want to be the first to uncover it."

"I want to help," Krista said, a little too enthusiastically.

"You want to break into a funeral home?" I raised my eyebrow, leaning back in my seat.

She nodded. "And I want to do more than just play the driver this time."

Gina chimed in. "The body is at Martin's Funeral Home. How about we swing by this afternoon to gather some intel? We can scout the place for any security cameras outside and check the sturdiness of the doors."

I drummed my fingers on the worn wooden table, lost in thought. "It would really help if we could get a glimpse of the interior layout too."

Dominic pulled his phone from his back pocket

and began scrolling through it with swift, practiced movements. "Looks like there's a viewing this afternoon from two to four for a woman named Betty Stevenson," he announced.

"Who's that?" Krista asked.

Dominic shook his head. "Says here she was eighty-two and lived in Gettysburg her entire life. She had five kids and fifteen grandchildren. "He whistled. "That's a lot of kin."

"We could say she was a friend of Mom, and we are paying our respects," Gina suggested. My grandmother passed away several years ago. She was a vibrant part of the community, so it wouldn't be surprising if she had crossed paths with Betty.

"Perfect," I said. "Gina and I can scope out the funeral home this afternoon. Then the three of us can return together tonight."

Dominic leaned back in his seat. "What about the sheriff?" he asked, his voice low and steady.

Krista tilted her head, confusion etched on her face. "What do you mean?"

Dominic's gaze grew serious as he replied, "If something goes wrong tonight and they end up calling the police, the sheriff will be on you like flies on shit."

I cringed. "Nice euphemism."

"It's true."

We fell into an uneasy silence, each of us lost in our own thoughts, the tension palpable. The sound of Gina's fingernails tapping rhythmically against the table was almost deafening. After a few moments, she stopped.

"I've got something planned for the sheriff."

Now I was worried.

We spent the next fifteen minutes discussing our plan for tonight's break-in. Just as we wrapped up our discussion, Sheriff Earl strode through the door, his head held high, and his chest puffed out like a rooster entering his domain. He marched directly to a table by the window, settling in with an air of self-importance, completely oblivious to our small group huddled at the rear of the restaurant.

Gina's lips twisted into a pout as she crossed her arms defensively over her chest. "Ugh, I forgot he was coming in today."

A smirk tugged at the corner of my lips. "I didn't." Pushing myself up from our table, I grabbed my thermal cup and, adopting my best Terminator impression, declared, "I'll be back."

With a stride of casual confidence, I approached the counter several stools down from the nearest diner, keeping my gaze subtly trained on Sheriff Earl. I waited patiently for the waitress to return after taking his order.

"Hey Sydney, What's up? Do you want some dessert?" she asked with a bright smile as she stepped behind the counter, pausing just across from me.

Indiah's mother owned the diner, and Indiah and I had been close friends since our high school days. Her father had run off many years ago with another woman, leaving Indiah to support her mother and manage the diner after graduation. With her long, chestnut hair cascading over her shoulders and warm olive skin, she always struck me as someone who could thrive in modeling or acting. Yet, it didn't always work out the way you would like. If it weren't for fate, I wouldn't have been standing here either.

I declined. "Maybe later. What did the sheriff order?"

She tilted her head slightly. "Same thing he gets every day. Bacon cheeseburger, fries, and a diet Coke." she rolled her eyes dramatically. "As if a diet soda will make up for the thousand other calories he's about to demolish."

"Excellent." I discreetly slid the thermos across

the counter towards her, keeping my voice low. "Can you slip these into his soda?"

"Sure," she responded without even pausing to inquire about the mysterious contents of the silver thermos.

With a smile, she slid the cup beneath the counter, carefully peeling back the lids. But as she peered inside, her expression shifted drastically. A frown creased her brow, and her eyes widened in surprise. "It's filled with ice," she exclaimed, disappointment etched across her features.

I nodded, a smirk playing on my lips. "Special ice."

"Earl thinks he deserves a free meal just because he's Sheriff." Indiah's face lit up like the joker. "I'm in for whatever happens."

Out of the corner of my eye, I spotted an older man perched at the far end of the counter. He was observing us intently, but as soon as our eyes met, he quickly averted his gaze.

The ice cubes clicked against the glass as she poured them in. She added the soda with a few swift movements, releasing a cascade of bubbles that surged to the surface with a lively fizz.

"Let me run in back and grab his sandwich."

All eyes at my table riveted to me as I returned.

"What did you do?" Gina asked anxiously, her anticipation was evident.

I gestured subtly toward the Sheriff seated across the room. "Watch and see," I replied, the thrill of my plan bubbling beneath the surface.

Though it felt like an eternity, probably less than a minute passed before Indiah approached the table with a tray carrying Earl's meal. Just like at work, every detail had been meticulously calculated, and now we could only wait for the grand finale to unfold.

Indiah placed the plate in front of Earl and reached for the glass. The door swung open just then, and Blake burst into the diner. He scanned the room, his gaze locking onto Earl. He crossed the space with purposeful strides, engaging the Sheriff in conversation. Indiah slowly removed the glass from the tray while listening to the conversation.

Unexpectedly, the Sheriff stood up from the wooden chair, the legs scraping against the floor with a harsh sound. He strode purposefully towards the door. To my horror, I watched Blake slide into the chair the Sheriff had just vacated.

"No," involuntarily escaped my lips.

Blake had a short conversation with Indiah, and then she walked away with her tray under her arm, her shoulders slumped in a resigned manner. She made her way to the counter and hastily deposited her tray. She rushed over to our table, urgency etched across her face.

"What happened?" I asked, my voice thick with anxiety.

"Blake told Earl that Mayor Westman wanted to see him immediately. Earl insisted that Blake could have his lunch since he hadn't touched it," Indiah said.

"Did you try to stop him?"

"I tried my best," Indiah insisted. "I offered to bring him anything he desired on the house. But he wouldn't budge, insisting the burger and soda were fine."

I dropped my head into my hands, overwhelmed by the unfolding disaster. This situation couldn't possibly have spiraled any worse.

CHAPTER 9

"What's in those ice cubes?" Indiah asked.

Everyone at the table looked anxious to know the answer. I leaned my head against the back of the booth. Lately, it seemed that if I didn't have bad luck, I would have no luck at all.

"I froze a Mentos inside each one of the ice cubes this morning."

The moment the words left my lips, every gaze snapped toward the glass brimming with soda, the bubbles swirling slowly to the surface.

Krista's hand flew to her mouth, her face a mixture of disbelief and excitement. "Oh my God. I saw what happens when you mix soda with mentos on a YouTube video."

"So have I," Dominic said as he whipped out his phone and pointed it towards Blake.

"Put that away." I urged. "If he sees you with that, and things go south, he'll know we had a hand in it."

"What can we do?" Krista asked.

Gina leaned in, her eyes darting around the room as if expecting someone to burst in at any moment. "What if you called Sean? He could reach out to Blake and drum up a reason for him to head back to the station."

Nodding, Krista pulled her phone from her purse

and dialed. "Hi honey," she said when Sean picked up. "I need you to do me a big favor. Call Blake and tell him to come to the station immediately." She paused. "I don't care what excuse you use. Just come up with something. I'll fill you in later." With that, she abruptly hung up, leaving no time for questions. All we could do now was wait.

Meanwhile, Blake remained unaware of the situation. With one hand clutching his phone, he was engrossed in whatever was playing on the screen. His free hand picked up his burger, and he took a bite. Then, he grasped his glass, bringing it to his lips for a sip.

We sat in silent anticipation, our eyes fixed on him as if observing the final moments of a countdown timer on the brink of detonation.

He raised the soda to his lips, and I could hear the sharp intake of breath from everyone at the table. He took a long sip, and I finally released the breath I had been holding as he set the glass back down with a soft thud.

"What's taking Sean so long?" I asked, the unease creeping into my voice.

"I don't know. He should have called by now." Just then, her phone chimed with a notification, cutting through the tense silence. She glanced at the screen, her brow furrowing slightly as she read the message.

"Uh-oh. Sean said Blake's phone is going straight to voicemail. He must have his notifications turned off while he's on break."

"Now what?' Indiah asked.

"Why don't you go over and talk to him?" Gina suggested, her gaze shifting to me. "You can flirt with him."

"Are you nuts? I would never do something like that. If I walk over there, he'll know something is seriously wrong."

We watched in tense silence as he took another

drink, the amber liquid swirling within the glass.

The thought of failing a mission so spectacularly gnawed at me. If I messed up this badly at work, they would drum me out of counterintelligence and reassign me to kitchen duty.

"Maybe freezing the Mentos deactivated their power," Gina suggested.

I prayed that was the case.

Blake's attention remained fixated on his phone, and he was already halfway through his burger. He popped a fry into his mouth and reached for his soda once more. Every time he lifted that glass, I cringed.

As he raised the frosty glass, the clinking ice danced within. With a casual tilt of the cup towards his lips, the ice must have shattered under the force which triggered a spectacular eruption. Soda surged forth like molten lava from a volcano, spraying out in an explosive cascade just inches from Blake's unsuspecting face.

Blake was completely absorbed in his phone, his attention ensnared by the glowing screen, when he was suddenly ambushed by a torrent of icy soda. The liquid shot towards him with an unexpected force, drenching his face and hair as if he had stood in the path of a relentless fire hose. Surprised, he coughed and sputtered, his grip faltering as the glass slipped from his fingers. The glass flew across the table and crashed against the corner, shattering into pieces that scattered onto the floor.

With wide eyes and a look of disbelief, Blake sprang to his feet, unintentionally knocking over his chair. The soda pooled around him, creating a three-foot-wide circle. It was a scene so comical that we struggled to stifle our laughter. As the hilarity of the moment settled over us, Indiah rushed over to Blake's side, concern mingling with amusement on her face.

"I think it's time for us to leave," I said. I threw enough money on the table to cover our tab and for a generous tip.

As we stood to leave, I noticed Blake caught our movements from the corner of his eye. His gaze snapped toward us. I managed a smile and gave him a casual finger wave, hoping to lighten the mood, but he wasn't having any of it. His face contorted with anger, his brows furrowing deeply as he glared at me, a storm brewing in his eyes. Without a word, he turned away from Indiah and stormed out of the diner, the door slamming shut behind him.

We all sat back down as the restaurant erupted into a roar of laughter as soon as the doors clicked shut. Unable to contain herself, Krista flopped across my lap, her body shaking with uncontrollable giggles that seemed to ripple through us all. Meanwhile, Gina was bent over the table, tears glistening in her eyes as she gasped for breath between fits of laughter.

I joined in, unable to resist the wave of laughter sweeping through the diner, yet a nagging thought crept into my mind. Would Blake retaliate? As the laughter began to subside into softer chuckles, I gestured for Indiah to come over, ready to settle the bill.

"Don't worry about the bill," Indiah said, her laughter still bubbling beneath her words. "Old man Remi paid your tab. He said he hadn't laughed this hard since his prize goat fell off the roof."

As I pondered the absurdity of his statement, I shook my head, realizing some questions were better left unasked. I reached across the table, picked up the cash, and handed it to Indiah.

"You did the hard work, so you deserve the money."

With her hands thrown up in playful protest, Indiah continued to chuckle. "No way! Like I told Blake, I have no clue what went wrong with the soda. There must be something malfunctioning with the dispenser."

"You're the best," I said as I slid out of the booth and headed out of the diner.

* * * *

Bodyworks was nestled on the corner of Grant Street. I was happy to see that it didn't have a glass front that looked into the gym. I have never understood gyms where anyone on the street could gawk at the members while they worked out. Who wants to be exercising while people on the street criticize your performance? I figured ego maniacs who thought their bodies were perfect were the only ones who wanted to work out in a fishbowl.

The guy standing behind the counter resembled one of those guys. Muscles rippled beneath his skin, and he looked like he could easily rival Schwarzenegger when he was in his prime. His neck was stout and thick, swallowed by the sheer bulk of his broad shoulders and beefy chest. It looked like his head was attached to his upper body, akin to a bobblehead.

As we entered the lobby, Dominic confidently strode over to the muscular figure and made the introductions.

"Biff, these are my friends Gina and Sydney."

Why was I not surprised the muscle-bound man before me was named Biff.

"Nice to meet you," he rumbled, his voice deep and gravelly as if he had swallowed shards of glass along with his protein shake that morning. "Are you interested in joining the gym?"

"Actually, we came to ask you about another member," Dominic said.

"Oh?" Biff's brow furrowed.

"Charlie Winchester," I continued. "He used to come here about a year ago. Do you remember him?"

Biff shook his head.

Gina leaned forward. "We were wondering if you could check how often he visited and if he spent a lot of time with anyone in particular."

Biff shook his head more firmly this time. "Sorry, I can't disclose that. My patron's information is confidential."

"But he's dead, so technically he's no longer a member here," Gina countered.

Biff's demeanor hardened as he crossed his arms tightly over his chest, the fabric of his white wife beater tank top straining against his muscular build. "Doesn't matter," he replied, his tone unwavering. "I respect my member's privacy and won't divulge their personal information, workout routines, or acquaintances to anyone."

I blew out my breath and looked around the lobby. It was small, with a reception desk at one end, the glass double entrance doors centered, and a modest evergreen tree occupying a planter at the other end. To the side, a wide doorway revealed the gym beyond, where I could see a man pedaling furiously on an exercise bike. Nearby, a woman struggled on an elliptical, her face flushed and weary, looking as though she might collapse at any moment from exhaustion. I shifted my focus back to Biff.

"So, there's no way you'll divulge what we need to know?" I asked, trying to gauge his expression.

"Not without a cop and a warrant," he replied curtly, his voice as unyielding as granite. "Now, are either of you interested in joining the gym?"

"I may be interested," Gina replied. "But I would like to look around first and try out a few machines."

Biff's gaze swept over Gina. Luckily, Gina decided to go casual today. She was wearing a pair of leggings with Van Goh's starry night printed on them. Her simple black T-shirt and comfortable sneakers completed the outfit. It was a look that could easily be mistaken for workout attire.

Biff must have appreciated her choice as he nodded in approval before turning his attention to Dominic. "Show your friends around," he instructed, his voice friendlier than before.

Then, his eyes landed on me, sizing me up with an almost appraising look. I wore denim cargo shorts that hung just above my knees, and my tattered combat boots added a rugged touch.

"I suggest you stick to just looking around today and resist the urge to try out any equipment," he advised.

I suppose I didn't quite fit the stereotype of someone prepared to dive into exercise. Even with my current outfit and my injuries, I was confident I could bench press a hundred pounds. In my prime, that number would have soared closer to one hundred sixty, but he didn't need to know my full capabilities.

As we entered the gym, a familiar blend of rubber and sweat flooded my senses. We paused beside the empty rowing machines. The man on one of the bikes continued to pedal vigorously, his expression focused. At the same time, the woman had seemingly vanished, likely retreating to the locker room to have a coronary in peace. Near the bench press, two men were engaged in a lively workout session. One was lifting a hefty barbell, and the other in a red tank top was his cheerleader yelling, "You the man!"

Gina leaned in close, her voice barely above a whisper as we gathered together. "I have a plan," she said, her eyes gleaming with determination. "The treadmills are off to the side. I can hop on the one in the corner, hidden from the view of the front lobby. I'll create a distraction that'll force Biff to leave his post. That'll allow Dominic to hack into the computer to get the information we need."

Whenever Gina came up with a plan, I felt a little nervous, but I couldn't find any faults with this one, so I nodded in agreement. "I'll stand in the doorway and get Biff's attention."

We fist-bumped, and I walked over to the doorway between the lobby and the gym. Dominic headed into the lobby towards the front desk. Biff's gaze shot to me as I leaned my back against the wall and propped my boot up on the wall behind me.

"I hate exercising," I said nonchalantly.

He nodded and shifted his attention to Dominic.

"I saw the coolest machine during my trip to Florida called an ab crunch machine," Dominic exclaimed. He leaned forward, resting his elbows on the desk, to capture Biff's full attention. "You should consider getting one."

I glanced back at Gina, who stood precariously on the treadmill, her feet securely planted on the metallic side rails instead of the moving conveyor belt. It appeared she had activated the machine, but rather than run, she just stood there. Drawing a deep breath, she let it out slowly, like a warrior preparing for battle. Her fingers gripped the side bars so tightly that her knuckles turned a shade of white.

Before I could fully comprehend her wild plan, she shifted her weight and placed one foot onto the speeding belt. But before her second foot could even make contact, the treadmill launched her backward with astonishing force as if she had been shot out of a cannon. The action was so swift that her body barely grazed the machine; only her forehead skimmed the underside as she was violently ejected into the dumbbell rack behind her.

The stand wobbled precariously before toppling over, sending the weights crashing to the ground with a loud bang that echoed like a thunderclap through the gym.

Biff glanced up sharply, his expression shifting

from focus to alarm. "She fell off the treadmill," I said, genuine concern lacing my voice.

Without hesitation, Biff darted around the desk and raced into the gym. I shot Dominic a quick thumbs-up and hurried after Biff.

Gina lay sprawled face down, her body awkwardly positioned with her legs draped over the overturned rack. She resembled a hapless Black Friday shopper who had been trampled in the chaotic rush of bargain hunters as the doors swung open.

The treadmill was still humming, running at maximum speed. The men from the bench press were now congregating around Gina, attempting to help her regain her footing.

"Are you alright?" Biff asked, his voice laced with concern as he powered down the treadmill.

Gina sat up and leaned over to clutch her ankle. "I twisted my ankle while running, which threw me off balance and made me fall."

I rolled my eyes at the drama unfolding before me.

Kneeling beside her, Biff gently examined her ankle. Gina caught my eye and shot me a wink over Biff's shoulder. Meanwhile, a vivid red rectangular mark adorned her forehead, where it hit the treadmill's moving belt.

"It doesn't feel broken. Let me get you an icepack." Biff stood up and turned his back to us, heading toward the lobby.

"No," we exclaimed in unison.

He halted, surprise flickering across his face as he turned back towards us, his eyes wide with confusion.

"You don't need to go through the trouble," Gina insisted. "Just help me up, and I can walk it off."

Gina put on a theatrical display as she attempted to stand. When she grabbed his hand and was halfway up, she lost her grip and went tumbling back on her butt. Biff exchanged a knowing glance with the bodybuilder in the red shirt, who nodded in response. Together, they moved swiftly to her aid, each gripping her under the arms with careful strength, lifting her effortlessly into the air as if she were a feather.

"Oh my," she said as she dangled momentarily in the air.

They carefully lowered her down until her feet touched the ground, but she took great care to avoid putting any weight on her injured ankle, balancing precariously on one leg.

"Could you help me to my car?" she added, batting her eyes at Biff, causing mine to swoop up to the ceiling again.

With a gentle but supportive gesture, Biff slipped his arm beneath hers, allowing her to lean on him for stability as she slowly hobbled towards the entrance.

"As soon as you get home, take two aspirin and put ice on your ankle. Elevate the leg and stay off it the rest of the day," Biff advised as Gina limped towards the door using him as a crutch.

As we entered the lobby, I spotted Dominic leaning casually against the front door as he tapped away on his phone.

"Sorry, I had an important call I had to take," he lied. "Did I miss anything?"

Gina dropped Biff's arm. "Thanks for your help. Sydney can help me from here."

Biff's frown deepened, worry lines etched into his forehead as he studied Gina's pale expression. "If your ankle starts to swell, wrap it. Call me if you need anything." Beneath his protective demeanor, unease lingered, likely stemming from worries of a lawsuit since Gina wasn't a facility member and hadn't signed any contract or waiver.

"She'll be fine," I reassured, taking her arm to guide her towards the exit.

Gina continued to stagger along until we were outside. As soon as we were out of view, she dropped my arm and strode towards the cars, her pace now even and assured.

"I see that your ankle has miraculously healed," I smirked. "Are you out of your mind? Why on earth would you step on a speeding treadmill?"

Dominic's eyebrows shot up in surprise as the realization dawned on him about the unconventional distraction we had just escaped.

Gina shrugged. "When people on TikTok fall off of a treadmill, it always draws a big crowd."

"Those are blooper videos. Those people do it accidentally."

"Whatever," Gina replied. "It caused the distraction we needed, didn't it?" She reached up to feel the tender red mark on her forehead, wincing slightly as her fingers brushed against the skin. "Ouch! I think I got a brush burn."

I sighed heavily.

"So, how often did Charlie go to the gym?" Gina asked.

"He didn't," Dominic said as he leaned against his sleek Porsche, its glossy exterior catching the sunlight.

"What do you mean?" I asked, confusion flickering across my face.

"No evidence or registration was showing that Charlie had ever been a gym member."

Gina frowned; frustration etched on her features. "After everything I went through, we're back to square one?" she asked, her voice tinged with disappointment.

"Sounds like it," Dominic replied.

Gina glanced down at her watch. "We have to get

ready to go to Meadow Springs."

"I'll do some digging into the employees tonight," Dominic promised as he slid into his car. With a rev of the engine, he drove off.

.

CHAPTER 10

After a brief stop at the house to change into more suitable funeral attire, we pulled into the nearly full parking lot of the funeral home. Gina stepped out of the car; her figure draped in a form-fitting black dress. She ran her fingers down the fabric, smoothing out any wrinkles. Casting a quick glance in my direction, she raised an eyebrow.

"You could've at least worn a dress," she remarked.

I gazed up at the crystal blue sky. "I don't see any pigs flying," I replied with a smirk.

"Very funny."

I glanced down at my black leggings and matching t-shirt. "At least I'm dressed in the appropriate color."

"When you die, I'm putting you in a bright pink dress. Something that will really stand out."

I couldn't help but laugh. "Who said I was dying first?"

"With the way you're running around the globe pretending to be an action hero like GI Jane, it's obvious you'll be the one to go first."

"Ha. Who are you kidding?" I scoffed. "At the rate you're going, you'll manage to blow yourself up long before I even think about kicking the bucket."

She paused, her expression turning contemplative for a heartbeat as if she were weighing the truth in my words. "Maybe you're right. Let's get going."

As we strolled across the asphalt expanse of the parking lot, I noticed the sleek, metallic cameras mounted at both corners of the building, their lenses poised toward the vehicles and pedestrians below. "I see cameras at each of the corners of the building."

Gina added, "There's one at the corner of the door too," just before she stumbled, her ankle wobbling precariously. She instinctively reached for my arm, steadying herself as she regained her balance.

"What possessed you to wear heels?" I asked, glancing down at her black sequined stilettos. I couldn't shake the thought that she had enough trouble navigating even in flat shoes. With those three-inch stilettos, she would be a nightmare.

"I look great in these shoes."

"When was the last time you wore them?"

"This is the first occasion I've had to wear them since I bought them."

That was comforting.

As we reached the sleek, black SUV parked beneath the expansive overhang, she released her grip on my arm. The vehicle was longer than most, its tinted rear windows nearly blending into the darkness of the night. The back door stood open, so we peeked inside.

Inside, the interior was surprisingly spacious. It featured a long wooden floor with black rollers that stretched from the rear to the front seats. Folded-up metal shelves lined each side.

"They use SUVs for hearses now?" I asked.

"I guess they are less intimidating to people as they drive past."

As we stepped into the hall, we were met by a vast sea of people wearing solemn black attire. It was an ocean of unfamiliar faces that seemed to blur into one another. We weaved through the crowded space until we reached a room on our right. Outside the door, I spotted a familiar figure amidst the sea of black.

"Chloe, right?" I said to the woman who was wearing a vibrant shade of purple, a stark contrast to the traditional black.

She nodded. "Hi. I remember you both from Stylish Pooch. We're still laughing about what happened to Lucinda."

"What are you doing here?" Gina asked.

"I work here part-time," Chloe replied, her tone steady as she adjusted the collar of her purple shirt. "I'm responsible for doing the hair and makeup on the deceased. I was checking on Mrs. Stevenson's makeup before I headed out."

"You don't mind working on dead people?" Gina asked in disbelief.

Chloe shook her head, a soft smile gracing her lips. "Not at all. It brings me joy to know that I can help make them look beautiful one last time." With that, she turned and slipped away, disappearing into the crowd.

I gazed through the doorway of the viewing room, my eyes taking in the burgundy carpet that muffled sound with each step. To my right were a few scattered couches along the wall. In the center of the room stood meticulous rows of folding white chairs, some already occupied by mourners whose expressions were a mix of grief and remembrance.

To my left, a dark-stained wooden casket, crafted with intricate gold accents, rested atop a pedestal draped in purple velvet that cascaded to the floor. The air itself felt dense, as if the collective grief of the mourners had collected into a tangible cloud that you could feel but not touch.

We approached the casket as if to pay our respects

to the woman inside. She was a sizable figure, dressed in a deep plum purple dress.

"No cameras in the hall or this room," I whispered in Gina's ear as we stood beside the casket.

"Maybe the security cameras are only stationed at the entrances."

Just then, two older women approached, their expressions etched with grief. One of them let out a wail as she clutched a crumpled tissue to her eyes. "I can't believe Betty is gone," she said, her voice trembling. "She made the best pumpkin pie in town."

"At least she looks peaceful," the other woman remarked softly.

I bit back the urge to roll my eyes as I ushered Gina back into the hallway. I've never quite grasped why people feel the need to praise the appearance of someone in a casket. They rave about how serene someone looks or how they've never appeared more beautiful. But the truth was, they're dead and undeniably look it. No amount of makeup or careful positioning could alter that reality. The only consolation you could cling to was hoping their spirit had found its way to the right place.

"I wish we could explore the rest of this place," I murmured.

"You can," Gina said, tilting her head sideways.

I turned around and caught sight of John Martin exchanging pleasantries and shaking hands with one of the mourners.

I groaned.

"Come on," Gina urged. "Flirt with him and see if you can persuade him to give you a tour?"

"I don't flirt," I replied flatly, crossing my arms defensively.

"You flirted with the Brigadier in Paris when you had to."

I shot her a glare. "Once again, getting ourselves

arrested for prostitution."

"Anyone could have made that mistake," she replied defensively. "He looked just like the guy in my picture - our mark."

"His hair wasn't even the same color," I protested.

"No matter. Go and talk to him. I'll wait here," she said.

She nudged me toward John, who was standing a few paces away. I inhaled deeply, attempting to embrace a more feminine sway as I approached him. Behind me, I could hear Gina's muffled giggle, and I gave her the finger behind my back.

When John spotted me approaching, his face lit up with a radiant smile. While my walk may not have possessed the elegance of a runway model, it was certainly enough to keep him from turning tail and fleeing.

"Sydney, what brings you here?" he asked.

"Betty was a family friend," I lied. "I saw you and thought I would come over and say hi."

"Well, I'm happy to see you."

"Betty looks so calm and peaceful," I continued, struggling to maintain composure as I forced myself to say the words. "And that purple dress looks great on her." The compliment felt heavy on my tongue, but I smiled nonetheless.

"It does," he said with a sly smile. "Do you want to hear a secret?"

I opened my mouth to reply, but he continued.

"Her daughter was adamant that it was Betty's favorite dress, insisting she had to be buried in it. It was painfully evident that Betty hadn't worn that dress in over a decade, and despite our best efforts, we couldn't manage to get it on her."

"What did you do?" I asked, my curiosity piqued.

"We cut in down the back?"

"You're kidding." I covered my mouth with my hand to hide my smile.

His eyes sparkled. "Nope. We wrapped her up in it, just like a pig in a blanket."

I burst into laughter, the absurdity of the situation overwhelming me, and he joined in, our shared amusement echoing in the room. Once the laughter subsided, I collected my thoughts and redirected the conversation back to the matter at hand.

"This is a nice place," I remarked, glancing around with feigned interest, though I mentally chastised myself for such an awkward comment. Describing a funeral home as 'nice' felt utterly distasteful- ick. To my relief, he seemed oblivious, beaming at my observation.

"Thanks, let me show you around." He placed his hand on the small of my back and guided me down the hall away from the viewing room. Out of the corner of my eye, I spotted Gina watching us and gave her a thumbs-up.

We paused in front of a set of double doors. He swung them open, revealing a room that mirrored the one I had just departed.

"This is our second viewing room," he said as we moved forward down the hall.

As we walked down the corridor, I noticed a chocolate-brown metal door standing off to the side, its surface gleaming under the overhead lights. There was a keypad beside the door and a sign that boldly displayed, 'No admittance. Authorized personnel only.'

We continued to the end of the hallway, where he paused to open a door, revealing a room that exuded a sense of purpose. In the center stood a neatly organized desk and a computer that flickered gently.

To one side, a door with a small window offered a glimpse of the outside world, indicating an access to the side of the building.

"This is my office," he announced proudly.

"Very nice," I said, forcing enthusiasm into my voice. I glanced around the room quickly, but my attention was drawn to the door we had just passed in the hallway.

"But what's behind that door?" I asked, my finger pointing towards the other entrance.

"The morgue."

Bingo.

I clamped my hands together and bounced lightly on my heels, trying to display enthusiasm. "I have always wanted to see a morgue," I exclaimed, my voice infused with excitement as I attempted to mask the eye roll I felt bubbling up inside me at my act of flirting. "They look so fascinating on TV. Can you show me the morgue?"

"I don't know." His smile faltered as uncertainty danced in his eyes.

"Please." I urged, gently placing my hand on his forearm, my lashes fluttering in an attempt to charm him. I knew I could flirt with the best of them when given the right motivation.

His smile returned. "Why not. There aren't any autopsies scheduled today."

I was surprised. "You do autopsies here?"

"Well, not personally," he clarified, a hint of pride in his voice. "But, yes, autopsies are performed in our morgue. Our funeral home serves a dual purpose as the county morgue. Whenever an autopsy is required, the body and the coroner come here. It's the same for anyone who passes away at home or in an accident. They come here first until the family decides which mortuary to choose. More often than not, they opt to stay with us. We receive three times more business than the other funeral home in town."

He punched in a sequence of four numbers on the keypad, triggering a sharp beep followed by the unmistakable sound of the door unlocking.

John turned the handle and opened the door, revealing a short passage leading into a spacious room. The walls were a stark, clinical white, and the concrete floor appeared cold and uninviting. Despite the harsh fluorescent lights that hung overhead, illuminating the space, dampness prevailed, giving the room an eerie, oppressive vibe.

Two stainless steel tables stood in the center of the room, their polished surfaces gleaming faintly under the harsh overhead lights. A black body bag occupied one table. At the far end was an open garage door. The opposing wall, constructed entirely of steel, featured six large doors that resembled the heavy lids of ice chests. Each one could hold a lifeless form within its chilling confines. They looked exactly like the body storage freezers often depicted in crime dramas.

Next to the vacant table rested the silver casket that had been the focus of this morning's grave excursion. Most of the dirt had been cleaned away. The casket was placed on a steel gurney, which had been lowered almost to the floor. The air was filled with a sharp, pungent blend of vinegar mingled with the faint, musty scent of decaying pickles. The stench was so pungent it caused me to wrinkle my nose.

"What's that smell?" I asked. I had expected the scent of decomposing bodies, but instead, the air was thick with the smell of something that had sat in a jar in a refrigerator for too long.

"That's formaldehyde," John replied. "Let me show you around." As we walked over to the metal wall adorned with the cooler door, I scanned the room, noting the absence of cameras or motion detectors.

"This is everyone's favorite part of the morgue," John said as he pulled one of the metal drawers out with a smooth motion, akin to a file in an office cabinet. The cold air hit me as soon as the drawer opened, and I let out a breath that floated in front of me in the frigid air.

"This, of course, is the freezer where the bodies are stored until the funerals. The exam tables are for the autopsies," he explained, gesturing towards an open doorway. "Embalming is done through there, and our supplies are also stored in that area."

"Where does the open garage door go to?" I began making my way over.

"Out back."

Stepping outside, I turned to appraise the building's exterior. No security cameras were mounted above the garage door, but a keypad access system was installed beside it. I peered around the corner of the building and spotted the door that led into John's office. Just as I pivoted back to question John about the absence of security cameras, a black truck rumbled into the driveway and came to a halt right in front of the door.

The man who emerged from the vehicle was a sight to behold. Towering over six and a half feet, his presence was both imposing and unsettling. His hair was short and stringy, and his eyes, set deep within dark sockets, seemed to capture the haunting emptiness of an old, forgotten grave. Despite his considerable height, he had a lanky stature, his skin a ghastly shade of gray, reminiscent of death itself. He reminded me of Lurch from the Addams Family.

He approached us slowly, and I half-expected him to say, "You rang?"

"Sydney, this is Rocco Salvino, our mortician. He handles all the real work around here."

Rocco nodded, his movements reminiscent of a character from a horror film, as he made his way toward a heavy metal door set into the wall. The hinges creaked as he swung the door open, revealing a dimly lit interior before he stepped inside.

"I need to get him to oil those hinges," John said. "That room is the crematory. Would you like to take a look inside?"

Ick again. I had no interest in seeing where bodies were burned. I had already gathered all the information I needed, and my mind was busy piecing together a meticulous plan for the break-in scheduled for tonight.

"No, I'm good," I said my eyes involuntarily darting to the exit door anxious to leave.

He misinterpreted my signal. "I forget that not everyone is used to seeing all the death that I do. It can be rather startling to some."

He took my arm and guided me back down the corridor, leading me through the locked door. The hallway was nearly empty as everyone had filtered into the viewing room. As we made our way, John regaled me with tales about the history of funeral homes.

"Did you know," he began, a glint of excitement in his eyes, "that back in the seventeen hundreds, they actually had a special room designated for the deceased? They would keep the body there for several days to ensure they were truly dead."

"Fascinating," I replied, my gaze drifting around the viewing room in search of Gina. My eyes finally settled on her as she stood by the casket engaged in a conversation with a dwarf, or little person, or whatever politically correct term was proper to use these days to describe a man under four feet tall. He was animated, gesturing passionately as he spoke, his hands dancing through the air.

Gina listened attentively, nodding along with a warm smile. She then turned and strode to the front row of chairs, deftly removing one from its place. She helped the little man onto the chair, positioning it right in front of the casket to give him a better view of the scene within.

He balanced on his tiptoes, holding onto the edge

of the casket, straining to catch a glimpse of its contents. Suddenly, he shifted his foot, and the chair decided to fold up, pitching him forward. My eyes widened as I saw the chair kick out from under him and crash to the ground.

Chapter 11

"They attached bells to the dead person's wrist so they would be alerted in case the person was moving around and not dead."

I caught John's words drifting towards me as I stood frozen, watching the bizarre spectacle unfold before my eyes like a bad movie. The small man dangled awkwardly from the edge of the casket, his legs thrashing wildly in the air, emitting high-pitched screams like a three-year-old.

"Excuse me," I said to John, then turned to head into the room, but I was too late.

Gina hurried to assist, but as she did, her ankle twisted sending her crashing to the ground. To steady herself, she grasped the man at his waist. He remained determined, clutching the casket tightly as Gina pulled him down with her. Their combined weight proved too much for the fragile structure. It swayed precariously on its stand, teetering back and forth before finally tumbling off the pedestal with a resounding thud.

An eerie silence fell over the room, every breath held as onlookers processed the unfolding scene. The casket clattered onto its side, and a few gasps echoed as an unexpected figure emerged. With a dramatic roll, Betty tumbled out of the casket, her dress cascading away from her as she landed several feet in front of the astonished front-row audience.

Without her dress, she laid there in a red lace lingerie that looked like it came from Victoria's Secret magazine, except I didn't think they made undergarments that large. Without warning, a loud and resounding fart escaped from Betty, shattering the stillness of the room. Several women gasped in shock while one unfortunate soul fainted, collapsing to the floor right beside Betty. A few elderly mourners quickly knelt down in an attempt to carefully pull the fallen woman's dress from beneath three hundred pounds of dead weight, but it wouldn't budge.

The atmosphere was a mix of chaos and disbelief; some onlookers let out startled screams, while others wiped away tears of laughter or shock. A few reached for their cellphones, eager to capture the moment and ensure that this unforgettable incident would be forever immortalized on social media.

I rushed into the room, seized the velvet cover from the pedestal, and threw it over the body. Luckily, Gina and the man had been thrown to the side, so they weren't crushed as the casket came tumbling down. Gina sat on the ground, holding the heel of one shoe in her hand. I reached out to help her, but before I could say anything, a middle-aged woman stormed up to us.

"Look what you did!" she screamed. "You desecrated my mother's funeral, and I don't even recognize you. Who are you?"

Gina and I exchanged a fleeting glance before bolting for the front door. I raised my hand in a quick wave at John as we burst out into the sunlight. I sprinted toward the car. Gina, half running and half wobbling on one precarious heel, struggled across the parking lot when suddenly, two men emerged from the building, hot on her trail.

The engine of the Mustang roared to life as I spun the wheel, blasting out of the parking space. I maneuvered toward where Gina was still struggling to reach me. Just as she lunged into the passenger seat, I hit the gas before the door fully closed behind her.

She instinctively grabbed the overhead handle as I sharply turned onto the road, the tires squealing in protest.

"We should have had a getaway driver," she panted.

"That's all you can say?" I shot back.

"The man wanted to see his dead aunt one last time."

I shook my head as I pressed the accelerator, surging onto Washington Street, the funeral home fading behind us.

* * * *

We walked through Meadow Springs unlocked employees' entrance five minutes before our shift started. Gina headed towards the janitor's closet to gather supplies while I headed straight towards the nurses' station.

As I strode down the corridor, the rhythmic clicking of keys on a keyboard echoed in the stillness, drawing my attention to the office just ahead. I peered inside, where I found Shirley hunched over her desk, the computer screen's glow illuminating her weary features. When she finally glanced up, her silver-framed glasses slipped slightly down the bridge of her nose, and she offered a smile.

"Good evening, Sydney," she greeted.

I gave a quick wave in return as I continued down the hall. I knew that if Shirley remained at her post much longer, Gina would have to initiate our carefully devised distraction plan.

I instinctively brushed my fingers against the

pocket of my navy scrub top, feeling the reassuring outline of the thumb drive—what Dominic whimsically dubbed the "rubber ducky." Gina and I silently agreed to hold off on our plan for at least an hour. As the minutes slipped by, I settled into the nurse's station, engaging in light conversation with Bridgett.

After a while, a young woman strolled casually behind the desk and plopped down in a chair next to me. She pulled out her phone from her pocket, her fingers flying over the screen as she scrolled through an endless stream of social media videos.

"Sydney, this is Eryn," Bridget introduced.

Eryn appeared to be in her early twenties, her long chestnut hair swept back into a ponytail. She barely glanced up from her phone.

"Hello," I said, trying to engage with her, but my greeting went unanswered. Turning back to Bridget, I asked, "Where's T.J. tonight?"

"It's his night off," Bridget replied.

I turned back to Eryn." How long have you been working here?"

"About a year," she answered flatly, her eyes glued to the screen.

"Do you like working here?"

With a slight shrug of her shoulders, she replied, "When people aren't asking me questions." Her tone made it clear that she preferred the solace of her phone over small talk.

"Don't mind her," Bridget said. "You know the new generation is addicted to their phones."

Without lifting her gaze from the screen, Eryn responded by sticking out her tongue.

We began our conversation casually, discussing the unpredictable weather and the latest happenings in the local news. As the initial awkwardness faded and we became more at ease with one another, I decided to delve deeper with some more personal inquiries.

"How often do residents pass away around here?"

Bridget looked taken back. "That's an odd question."

"It just seems like you'd form bonds with the residents after a while," I said softly. "It must be hard when one of them passes away, especially someone you've grown fond of."

She nodded, a hint of sadness crossing her face. "It is. Just last week, Mr. Choe choked on a piece of chicken. For a moment, I thought he was a goner. Luckily, Eryn managed to Heimlich him just in time."

Eryn, still engrossed in her phone, gave a thumbs up.

At that moment, an old man with a cane hurried past the desk—well, hurried as fast as he could go. Although a one-year-old toddler just learning to walk would have probably moved faster. Following him at a snail's pace was an old woman, gripping a walker that squeaked loudly with each turn of its front wheels. Bright yellow tennis balls were affixed to the bottom of the back legs.

"Slow down, Henry. You can't get away from me," She called out breathlessly, causing the man to quicken his pace just a little.

Bridget smiled. "That's Gale. She's on the hunt for her next husband. Which would make her fourth husband."

"Fifth," Eryn chimed in.

Good Lord, I struggled to fathom how anyone could tolerate a partner long enough to marry them even once, let alone five times. Just then, the sound of ringing interrupted my thoughts, as both Bridget and Eryn fished their phones from their pockets.

Bridget's expression darkened as she glanced at the screen. "It's Sam."

Eryn scoffed. "He's all yours and Sydney's. I'll take Donna tonight."

Bridget pressed a button on the phone. "I'll be right there, Sam," she said with a sigh. Rising from her chair, she gestured for me to follow. "Come on, Sydney. It's time to introduce you to the more... entertaining aspects of the job."

We made our way down the lit hallway toward apartment twenty. Bridget knocked lightly on the door before pushing it open. The moment we stepped inside, I was greeted by the sight of the old geezer from the night before in the navy robe.

"Sydney, this is Sam," Bridget introduced. "He has a little trouble getting in and out of the shower, so we're here to help him." She leaned closer to me, her tone dropping to a whisper, "Watch out for his hands."

Sam flashed me a wide smile that lit up his face, raising his eyebrows in quick succession.

Oh, hell no – two shots of whiskey weren't nearly enough to wipe away the unwanted memory that replayed in my mind of his miniaturized Mr. Winky. I would have to bleach my brain to erase the image of him bathing naked in front of me. There was no way I was going to help with shower time.

I found myself desperately crafting an excuse to escape the apartment when, suddenly, a deafening bang erupted from outside.

Instinct kicked in, and I crouched low behind the refrigerator. As I reached behind my back, I remembered with a sinking feeling that my trusty nine-millimeter wasn't within reach. Gina had insisted I leave it in the car, saying it would look suspicious if anyone spotted me with it. I silently cursed my decision. Sam looked so startled that he fanned himself and plopped down in the chair beside him.

"What was that?" Bridget exclaimed, her voice

tinged with panic as she bolted out the door.

Without hesitating, I followed her to the nurse's station. Just then, Shirley rushed down the corridor, her heels clicking against the polished floor as she hurried out of the office.

"Does anyone know what that noise was?" she asked a note of urgency in her tone.

We all exchanged bewildered glances and shook our heads. Gina was nowhere in sight, and I suspected the loud bang was her distraction.

"We need to check on the residents," Shirley instructed. "Bridget and Eryn, you two check the rooms upstairs. Sydney and I will check down here."

Bridget and Eryn quickly made their way to the elevators.

"Sydney, you take the east wing while I handle the north and south."

Once Shirley vanished around the corner, I hurried down the passageway toward the office. In her haste, Shirley had left the computer logged in, and I seized the moment to slip the thumb drive into the port. To my dismay, nothing happened, the screen remained blank. I quickly texted Dominic.

"Trust me, it's working." The reply came swiftly. I shot a glance at the clock ticking on the wall. Pacing behind the desk, I felt the weight of our plan resting on the thumb drive. Time seemed to stretch out as I waited, every instinct screaming at me to hurry. I stood behind the desk, my fingers wrapped tightly around the thumb drive as time passed. A piercing shout echoed down the hallway as I yanked it from the computer.

"Fire!"

I bolted out of the office, racing down the corridor. In the vestibule near the main entrance, a trashcan was engulfed in flames. The fire crackled and popped while thick black smoke billowed upward, swirling around me and stinging my eyes.

Shirley and Bridgett stood frozen in place, their faces a mix of shock and confusion, at a loss of what to do. Just then, I spotted Gina sprinting up the hall, clutching a fire extinguisher like a lifeline.

She gripped the handle tightly, yet she neglected to secure the nozzle in her haste. With a sudden burst of pressure, the nozzle whipped around wildly, unleashing a torrent of white foam that splattered against the walls. I instinctively tried to dodge the chaotic spray, but it was too late; the white, frothy foam struck me squarely in the center of my chest.

Gina grabbed the nozzle, holding on tightly this time, and aimed it at the flames. She unleashed a powerful stream of foam that surged over the fire, smothering it in mere seconds. Meanwhile, Shirley swung open the door, letting a rush of fresh air in and letting out the smoke before it could trigger the fire alarm.

"What's going on tonight?" Bridget asked in exacerbation.

Shirley shook her head. "I don't know, but it can't possibly get any worse."

Eryn appeared around the corner, her expression grave. "I wouldn't take that bet," she cautioned as she approached. "While checking on the residents, I found Pearl lying in bed. I think she might be dead."

Shirley sighed. "Let's go check on her. Sydney, grab a towel from the linen closet on your way by to wipe off that foam."

I sprinted towards the closet and quickly snatched a towel from the rack before entering the elevator. As the doors slid shut, I hurriedly brushed off the excess foam that clung to my skin. Despite my efforts, a large wet spot marred the middle of my chest, and my arms felt sticky from where the foam had landed.

Once we entered the apartment, we headed

straight for the bedroom, with Gina trailing closely behind me. Pearl lay on the bed as if she were sleeping. She appeared pale, but her skin had not yet taken on that sickly gray hue that often envelops the dead.

I moved around the far side of the bed while Shirley placed her fingers on Pearl's neck, searching for a pulse that would not come. As I cast my gaze toward the pillow beside Pearl's head, something caught my attention. A subtle yet distinct indentation now marred the once-fluffy cushion. I reached out and ran my hand over the indentation. I glanced at Gina, who stood nearby with an arched eyebrow, conveying a mixture of concern and intrigue.

"She's gone," Shirley uttered softly. "Bridget, call her next of kin. Eryn, contact the funeral home to come take her away."

"Aren't we going to do CPR?" I asked, hoping they would initiate it. I could barely remember the steps, let alone the ratio of breaths to chest compressions.

"No, Pearl was a DNR," Shirley said.

I recalled that DNR meant do not resuscitate, but I wondered how Shirley knew Pearl was one.

"You remember that she's a DNR?" I asked.

"Most of the residents are," she replied. "I know it's difficult when one of them passes, but we have to face the reality that they're elderly. Death is a natural part of their lives." She glanced at me with concern and frustration, noting how I was still damp, reeking of the chemicals from the fire extinguisher foam. "Take the rest of the night off. Gina, can you clean up the mess in the foyer before you leave?" Shirley turned and exited the room.

I waited anxiously in the car for almost an hour. Finally, the door swung open, and Gina slid into the driver's seat.

"What took you so long?" I inquired, trying to

mask my impatience as she fumbled with the keys, finally starting the engine with a sputter.

"You wouldn't believe the struggle it was to clean up the mess left by the fire extinguisher foam. It was like trying to scrape dried glue off the walls. It was a sticky, stubborn nightmare. I'm not sure I got it all off."

"What did you use to cause the loud bang?"

"An M80," came the casual reply.

My jaw dropped open. "You set off an M80 inside an apartment building filled with retirees. You're lucky half of them didn't keel over from heart attacks. What if it would have damaged something when it went off?"

"Relax," she said casually, her voice betraying no worry as she gestured dismissively. "I chucked it into a metal trash can."

I fixed her with a stern glare. "Would that be the trash can that was engulfed in flames?"

"How was I to know it would start a fire? It's just supposed to go boom."

I lowered my head into my hand, shaking it slowly.

"What do you think happened to Pearl?" Gina asked.

"I don't know. The pillow beside her was sunken and still slightly warm in the middle."

"Do you think someone was sleeping beside Pearl when she died?"

I frowned. "Or used the pillow to suffocate her."

Gina's mouth dropped open in shock, forming a perfect 'O' as the idea took hold. "Do you think it's Eryn since she found the body?"

"She would certainly be the most likely suspect. Although, she seems rather young to be a cold-blooded killer."

"You never know. Look at the Menendez brothers," Gina pointed out.

True. Her comment hung in the air, a chilling reminder of how appearances could be deceiving.

Chapter 12

Krista pulled into the driveway at midnight. I dashed upstairs and quickly tied my hair back into a ponytail. When I returned, I found Gina already settled into the passenger seat of Krista's black SUV. We rode in Krista's ride instead of Gina's vintage Mustang, since it was bright, canary yellow, and screamed for attention. With my motorcycle parked at the house, Krista's SUV was the perfect choice for our late-night excursion.

As we glided onto the quiet street, Gina turned to me, her expression serious. "We have a stop to make before heading to the morgue," Gina said.

Following her lead, Krista navigated through town until we reached a seemingly ordinary Cape Cod-style home at the end of a quiet cul-de-sac. The street lay still, eerily quiet. Even the leaves seemed frozen in place without a whisper of wind.

"The cemetery is livelier than this place," I remarked.

"This is a family community," Gina replied. "Everyone's in bed by now."

The white house was dark with no interior lights on.

"Why are we stopping here?" I asked. "What's important about this place?"

"Nothing," Gina replied. "It's that house we're here for." Gina extended her finger to point down the road. Her gaze focused on a brick ranch house three doors down and across the street.

It wasn't the dwelling that captivated my attention. It was the white sedan with red and blue light strips adorning the roof. On the side door, the word "Police" was written in bold black letters.

I dreaded asking but knew I had to. "Whose house is that?"

"Can't tell you," Gina said.

"Why not?"

"Plausible deniability."

"It's not plausible deniability if I'm aiding you with whatever scheme you've concocted." I paused in the middle of my snit. "Wait a minute... this is Sheriff Earl's house, isn't it?"

I took her silence as confirmation. "Oh my God!" I exclaimed. "You're not old enough to play the senility card, but I am seriously questioning it. Do you realize what happens if he catches us here? He'll bury us under the jail."

Gina turned in her seat to face me. "Look, if something goes wrong tonight, you know as well as I do, his first stop will be my house."

"Nothing is supposed to go wrong," I reminded her.

"We both know that, but with us involved, that's wishful thinking. We need to take precautions to prevent the Sheriff from showing up."

Krista drummed her fingers on the steering wheel as I weighed our options. After what felt like an eternity, I sighed, "Fine."

I exited the vehicle and started across the street. Glancing over my shoulder, I spotted Gina struggling with a large black duffle bag. With a grunt, she heaved it out of the trunk, but it fell to the pavement with a loud thud that quickened my pulse.

"Could you be a little quieter?" I scanned the surrounding houses. Any disturbance might rouse the neighbors from their slumber and cast unwanted attention on us.

"Sorry, it's a bit heavy," she muttered as she began to drag the large bag behind her along the pavement.

I rolled my eyes in exasperation. "Let me help," I said, stepping forward to lift the other end. The weight was considerable, nearly pulling me off balance. "What on earth is it filled with? Bricks?"

She didn't answer, her focus intent as we made our way across the street. We crouched behind the police cruiser. Around us, a few houses had dusk-to-dawn pole lights, casting enough soft light for us to navigate.

We surveyed the front of Earl's house, scanning for any hidden cameras or motion-activated floodlights that might catch us in the act.

"I can't believe he has no security in front of his house. Not even a camera doorbell," Gina remarked.

"He probably thinks that no one is stupid enough to vandalize his property, considering he's the Sheriff."

A smirk played on Gina's lips as she shrugged. "Obviously, that's not true. Let's get to work."

She moved to the car's back tire and unzipped the duffle bag. I peered inside and was shocked. "It's full of bricks."

Gina nodded. She retrieved a jack from the bag and positioned it under the vehicle's frame. With a little effort, she cranked the handle, lifting the tire off the ground with a soft metallic creak.

"What are you planning to do?" I asked.

"I'm going to place bricks behind each tire, just enough to lift the car a few centimeters off the ground. The wheels will barely hover above the pavement, yet not so high that the Sheriff will notice when he comes out to his vehicle. When he tries to back out, he'll hit the gas, but nothing will happen; the tires will spin helplessly in mid-air." A mischievous giggle escaped her lips, and she quickly covered her mouth to stifle it.

"And if everything goes according to plan tonight and he doesn't get a call?" I asked, raising an eyebrow.

"He'll just think some kids played a prank on him."

We worked efficiently as Gina jacked up the car, and I carefully positioned the bricks with deliberate precision behind each tire. After we finished, Gina tossed the jack back into the canvas bag, which held a few remaining bricks. We hurried down the driveway. As we reached the end, Krista spotted us and pulled up in front of the house. I eagerly jumped into the passenger seat while Gina tossed the duffle bag into the back seat before sliding beside it.

"How'd it go?" Krista asked as we sped away from the scene.

"Let's hope the rest of our night goes as smoothly," I replied.

Gina leaned back in her seat. "I wish I could see his face when he gets into the car tomorrow and tries to move it."

"To see his expression would be absolutely priceless," I added, chuckling at the thought of the surprise waiting for him.

* * * *

We parked our car on a side street across from the funeral home. During our surveillance mission earlier, I had scanned the perimeter. To my relief, I noticed that there were no security cameras monitoring the side of the building where John's office door was located. This would be our entry point—quiet and unobtrusive. Our plan was to break in through there and then head down the hall to the locked door that led into the morgue.

"Are you sure you know the code to the locked door?" Gina asked for the second time.

"Of course I do," I replied confidently. "John didn't even bother to conceal it when he punched it in." I could still picture the casual ease with which he entered the code, completely unaware that it would be useful to us. Now, all that remained was to execute our plan and slip into the building unnoticed.

"He was just excited you were giving him attention," Gina remarked teasingly.

"Did he ask you out?" Krista kidded.

"Thank God no. Of course, it was thanks to Gina and the chaos she caused that I got to escape."

"You're welcome," Gina said.

"That wasn't in any way a compliment," I replied. Gina shrugged.

"Alright, Krista. You're the lookout. Text me if you spot anyone near the funeral home or, heaven forbid, any cops."

"I know, I know," Krista scoffed. "I'm always the lookout."

I shook my head. "Even if you wanted to break in, your outfit is not conducive to doing the job."

"What's wrong with my outfit? This shirt's a Versace."

I glanced at Gina, who was clad head to toe in sleek black attire like me. In stark contrast, Krista stood out in her bright red t-shirt, the name "Versace" emblazoned across her chest in shimmering silver sequins.

"You need to wear black. In case you didn't know, black is the official color for any nighttime burglary," I explained.

"Sorry if I'm not exactly used to living on the wild side," Krista shot back.

"You ready?" Gina asked, her voice tinged with

impatience as if eager to end the long-winded conversation. We climbed out of the car and made our way across the dimly lit street, hurrying toward the side door of the building. Fortunately, the parking lot was illuminated only by sparse pole lights at the front, leaving the side cloaked in shadows. The moon hung overhead, casting a silvery glow just bright enough to guide our footsteps on the uneven ground.

I crouched down to remove my lock pick from my boot. As I straightened up, I caught sight of Gina pulling on a pair of vibrant pink latex gloves.

"Pink, really?" I had always encountered latex gloves in their typical shades of natural yellowish-beige or dull blue, but I was completely oblivious to the fact that they came in different colors. This made me wonder why you would need more than one color choice.

"I got you new gloves, too," Gina said.

I shot her a wary glance. "If you even think of handing me a pair of pink gloves, I swear I'll shoot you where you stand."

She gave me a "whatever" look before handing me a pair of black latex gloves.

"Sweet." I slipped on the gloves and focused on the lock before me. Within moments, the lock yielded with a satisfying clunk, and the door swung open.

"I can't fathom why people don't use deadbolt locks," I whispered as we stepped into the office and closed the door behind us.

"Makes it easier for us," Gina responded.

She was right. With the door left unlocked behind us, we quickened our pace down the narrow hallway towards the morgue's entrance. I approached the keypad and tapped in the code. The soft beeping echoed in the silence, and the locks clicked open.

We stepped into the corridor and slowed our movements as we neared the end of the hallway.

Searching the shadows, I cautiously leaned forward to peek around the corner. The darkness loomed still and quiet, so I flicked the lights on.

The fluorescent bulbs flickered to life, illuminating the morgue before us. It appeared exactly as it had that afternoon, offering a sense of relief.

"Let's go," I urged, moving purposefully toward the gray coffin.

Gina, however, hesitated, her gaze fixed intently on the black body bag sprawled across the cold, stainless steel table. She reached out and lifted the tag that hung from the zipper's slide pull.

"It's Charlie," she announced.

"Really?" I replied, stepping closer to her side. Glancing down, I couldn't help but notice the bag's slight form. It was obvious that it could contain just bones.

"Let's take a look," she said.

Before I could utter a word, I heard the sharp hiss of the zipper parting. She grasped the side of the bag closest to us and yanked it open. As the bag sagged, the top half of an aged white skeleton emerged into view. The dark void of the hollow eye sockets stared back at us while the jawbone was detached entirely, giving it an eerie look. There was a round hole in the center of the skull right above the eyes. I ran my finger over the hole, feeling the smoothness of the edges.

"It's not hard to figure out how he died," I said.

"What caliber bullet are you thinking did the job?"

"Judging by the size of the hole, I would say it came from a forty-four magnum or a forty-five."

Gina zipped the bag shut. As we approached the casket, a faint noise drifted in from the corridor to the funeral home. It sounded like a bang followed by a muffled groan.

"Did you hear that?" I whispered.

Gina and I dropped into a crouch behind the casket. I pulled my gun out and aimed it toward the shadowy entryway. Gina opened her purse wide, rummaging through its depths in frantic silence before finally closing it with a sigh of frustration.

"I forgot my gun," she whispered.

"How do you forget your gun?" I shot back.

"I pulled it out to make space for other items, then forgot to put it back."

"What did you end up bringing?"

"Taser, handcuffs, throwing stars, grenade, water bottle, lighter, some dynamite, a bag of ch-"

"We're definitely going to need to have a serious conversation when we get home."

We quietly waited behind the casket, straining to catch any sound. I was sure I heard the faint rustle of footsteps coming down the corridor. Suddenly, Krista stepped into view.

"What are you doing here?" I asked.

"I wanted to be part of the action for once," she replied.

I shook my head and stood up to tuck my gun securely back into the small of my back, feeling the familiar weight settle against my spine.

"I hope you didn't open the door with your hand. You'll leave fingerprints all over it."

"I'm not stupid," she said as she joined us in front of the casket. "I used my shirt to open the door."

"Hand her some gloves," I said to Gina.

Gina rummaged through her bag and pulled out another pair of pink gloves. Krista eyed the gloves before her gaze drifted down to my hands which donned black gloves.

"Do you have any purple?"

I threw my hands up in exasperation. "This is not Paris fashion week."

Krista stuck her tongue out at me and took the gloves.

The casket lay on a silver metal gurney that was lowered almost to the ground. With a gentle tug, I lifted the lid, and it opened smoothly. Revealing the stillness within.

"Aren't these supposed to be locked?" Gina asked.

"I guess someone else was curious enough to look at the body," Krista replied.

"Maybe it was the coroner. After all, he did want to do the autopsy. Or maybe Sheriff Earl, just to be nosy," Gina suggested.

The body lay before us, draped in a sapphire blue dress that stretched to her ankles. Her face was now muddy gray, and the texture was deteriorating, with patches of skin starting to flake away like old paint on a wall. Her once lustrous white hair now appeared frail and sparse, with strands falling out.

"She looks like someone colored her with a gray crayon," Krista said. "OMG, look at that ring."

Evaline's hands rested at her sides. The left hand, the one furthest away from us, drew my attention to the third finger, where one of the largest rings I have ever seen sat. It boasted an antique gold band with a striking turquoise gemstone in the center encircled by diamonds.

Gina gasped, and her eyes widened in disbelief. "That ring must be worth a fortune. Who in their right mind would bury someone with something that valuable?"

"Some people think they can take it with them," I replied, glancing at the piece, which was glinting in the light.

"I want a closer look." Gina placed her hand on the open lid and leaned over the body, reaching out to touch the ring.

"Are you going to take that ring off her finger?" Krista asked in horror.

"Maybe," Gina replied, her focus on the prize.

"You are not stealing that ring," I said firmly.

"Calm down," Gina replied. "I just want to try it on."

Gina tugged lightly but the ring got hung up on the knuckle. "It's stuck."

"If you pull that finger off, it's going to cause a whole new kind of trouble," I told her.

Krista wrinkled her nose. "This is so gross."

"Fine, let me try one more time." Gina gave the ring one strong tug, but it didn't budge.

Unfortunately, Gina lost her balance and, with a gasp, toppled forward. She reached out in a frantic attempt to regain her footing, but it was no use. With a crash, she landed across the lifeless form in the coffin.

"Serves you right," I quipped, watching as Krista dramatically placed her palm against her forehead and began to perform the sign of the cross.

"Just help me out."

Gina pushed off the lifeless legs of the body. I reached out, gripping her shoulder firmly, helping her navigate out of the tight space.

As she stood up, Gina's eyes widened in surprise. "I never realized how squishy a body became after embalming," she remarked.

"What do you mean?" I inquired.

"When I fell on her, it felt like her thighs compressed all the way down."

I raised an eyebrow in skepticism. Carefully, I placed my hand over the smooth silk of her dress and pressed firmly against her thigh. Sure enough, my fingers sank into the soft flesh, leaving a clear indentation, and the leg felt squishy. When I withdrew my hand, the mark lingered for several moments, then gradually returned to the surface, eventually leveling with the other leg.

"That was weird and a bit unsettling," Krista said.

"I agree," I replied, trying to shake off the odd feeling. "It felt oddly soft, almost like foam." With Gina's assistance, we raised the hem of her dress, lifting it up to her waist so that we could look at her thighs. Running down the center of both upper legs were five-inch cuts closed with black sutures.

"What the hell," Gina said.

"I thought she hadn't had an autopsy yet?" Krista responded.

"She didn't. And even if she had, they wouldn't cut open the legs," I explained. I reached into my pocket and pulled out my folding knife, flicking it open with a practiced snap.

Krista's eyes widened, growing as large as saucers, her disbelief morphing into alarm. "What are you doing?" she gasped.

"I'm going to cut the sutures open and see what is going on inside her leg."

Krista's face turned a sickly shade of green. "I think I'm going to be sick." She sank down onto the cool ground, leaning against the casket. She buried her head between her knees.

"You could have stayed in the car," I reminded her.

I took my knife and ran it carefully along the sutures, feeling the tension of the threads as they gave way. The incision popped open, revealing an orange foam hidden within.

"That's definitely not a bone," Gina remarked, her brow furrowed in confusion. "What exactly is it?"

I pressed down on the oddly shaped object, feeling it yield beneath my fingertip. Its texture was soft and spongy.

"It looks like someone has swapped out the femur

bone with a small foam cylinder like a pool noddle."

"Why would anyone do something like that?" Gina asked.

"I have no idea," I replied, still baffled.

A sudden rumble of an engine pierced the stillness as it drew closer to the garage. The sharp squeal of brakes cut through the air, signaling that a vehicle had stopped just outside the heavy door.

"Crap, someone's here. Hide," I said.

Chapter 13

I slammed the lid down on the casket, the sound echoing in the room. My eyes darted around, frantically searching for a hiding place, but the options were limited.

"Let's hide in the freezer," Gina suggested. She dashed over to the wall-mounted freezer, yanking open one of the metal drawers. The stretcher creaked as it rolled out. Gina climbed onto the stretcher and laid down flat. "Push me in," she urged.

I pushed the cold metal drawer back in. It clicked shut, sealing her in the darkness.

Krista, standing a little ways back, crossed her arms defiantly. "I've had enough creepy for one day," she said, her voice edged with anxiety. "I'm not hiding in there."

"Come on." I sprinted across the room to flick the lights off just as I heard a car door slam shut. I was halfway back across the room when the garage door came to life with a groan and started to rise. I opened the door to the crematory and ushered Krista inside.

The crematory was completely dark, which was just what I needed to keep Krista from freaking out about our location. The room smelled of burnt matches, a reminder of the place's grim purpose. I cracked the door open enough to peek outside.

Moments later, a white minivan backed into the morgue. The engine's low rumble faded to silence as it came to a stop beside the casket.

Two figures, clad in black from head to toe, emerged from the vehicle, their faces hidden by ski masks. One pushed on the table's pedal, elevating the coffin to the van's level, while the other slipped around to open the back door.

Through the dim light spilling from the van, I caught the silhouette of a third person inside who reached out and grabbed the handle at the end of the casket. In seconds, the trio maneuvered the casket into the van. Once the task was complete, the two masked figures hopped back into the front seats, and in an instant, the van sped off into the night.

I burst out of the door and sprinted across the room, but the fleeing vehicle was too far gone for me to make out the license plate.

"Who steals a casket?" Krista asked, her eyes widening. "It's just like weekend at Bernie's," she exclaimed excitedly. "Maybe they're going to pretend she's still alive." She clapped. "To break into a bank account worth millions."

"I doubt it," I replied, smiling and shaking my head. "It was probably someone desperately trying to hide the truth about the missing bones."

I heard a tapping coming from the freezer. Without hesitation, Krista dashed to it. She pulled open the door and rolled Gina out.

"Burr. It's dark, cramped, and freezing in here," Gina whined. "This is the closest I ever want to get to dying." She looked around the room. "Where's the casket?" She hopped down from the stretcher and pushed the drawer back in.

Just then, Krista's phone buzzed. "Uh, oh," she said, frowning as she glanced at the screen. "It's Sean. It reads, "I don't know what trouble the three of you are causing, but the police are heading to the funeral home.""

As I peered through the open garage door, my gaze fell upon the shattered remains of the keypad, its plastic casing cracked and scattered across the pavement. Where it once hung, two wires, one green and the other red, were twisted together on the wall.

"They broke in when they stole the casket," I said.

"They must have triggered a silent alarm," Gina replied.

Without wasting another moment, we dashed toward Krista's SUV. I quickly slid into the driver's seat while Krista offered no resistance as she leaped into the backseat beside Gina, ready to spring into action. I accelerated away, the SUV jolting forward at a speed faster than it had ever traveled.

Two blocks down the road, the wailing of sirens cut through the night air, drawing closer towards us. With a swift maneuver, I pulled up alongside the curb, behind a bright red sedan. The engine's hum fell silent, and I switched off the headlights, plunging us into darkness. We all ducked down as a police car raced past, its sirens fading into the distance.

Once the siren's sound had dissipated into a mere squeal, I cautiously eased back onto the street. We made our way home in what felt like record time. Knowing that Sean was already aware of Krista's presence with us, we decided it was best for her to stay the night. She quickly texted Sean, claiming she had drunk too much wine and would be crashing at our place tonight.

After a whirlwind of the day, we were exhausted and figured it would be best to retire to bed. We decided to leave the dissection of the evening's chaos for the morning. I was not even sure my head had hit the pillow before I drifted off into a deep, dreamless slumber.

* * * *

I gradually awoke to the unsettling feeling of pressure against my chest that made it difficult to breathe. There was no pain, just unexpected heaviness that made me question whether it was a new symptom related to my injuries or from yesterday's activity. I took a deep breath, but it felt like my chest was resisting me.

As I slowly opened my eyes, I was startled to see two beady eyes staring back at me. In a reflexive motion, I sat up, accidentally knocking Cagney off my chest. She tumbled, landing unceremoniously on my lap. In protest at being so abruptly uprooted, she pecked my leg sharply before darting out of the room.

Glancing around, I spotted Lacey perched at the foot of the bed, and I could hear the soft, rhythmic sounds of snoring to my left. Wilbur was sound asleep beside me. I gently patted him on the head to wake him from his slumber. He let out a big yawn, stretching his limbs lazily before drowsily blinking his eyes open. He nestled his head comfortably in my lap.

"It's too early for petting," I said, shifting my gaze to Lacey. "Well?"

She responded by shaking her head, but before she exited the room, she squatted in the middle of the floor and laid an egg.

"That's it," I declared, surprising Wilbur as I threw the covers back, causing Lacey to hurry off. After I got ready for the day, I cautiously stepped to my bedroom door and peered down the hallway. To my relief, there was no sign of the deranged chickens or the dog. I swore if I stepped in any chicken poop on my way down the stairs, I was going to end them.

I followed a heavenly aroma to the kitchen. There, standing by the stove, was Dominic, his back turned to me as he skillfully pulled a pan from the oven. I was too exhausted to question how he managed to slip into the house this time, especially since I had secured the door lock the previous night.

"Where did the mischief makers go?" I asked, noticing the absence of chickens in the pantry.

"I let them outside," he replied, his attention focused as he carefully transferred flaky pastries from the hot pan to a waiting dish.

I attempted a nod to acknowledge his words, but in my weary state, I was sure I didn't succeed. I shuffled my way toward the coffee maker. My hand was halfway to the pot when I suddenly stopped in my tracks. Even through my barely opened eyes, something felt distinctly wrong.

"Where's the coffee pot?" I couldn't think of a crueler punishment than stealing someone's coffee.

"It's on the table on the front porch," he said. "It's such a lovely morning. I thought we could enjoy our breakfast outside today."

I followed him and the yummy-looking pastries out the door. "What did you make?" I asked, my stomach rumbling in anticipation.

"Apple turnovers."

My mouth began to water. As the door creaked open, I spotted Gina sitting in a white rocking chair next to the table with the coffee pot on it. I settled into the other rocking chair and poured myself a cup of the blissful brew. I savored several warm gulps before my gaze drifted to the plate of turnovers. I swiped one off the plate and took a bite. The crust was perfectly flaky, crumbling delicately at my touch, while the warm filling oozed with sweet, juicy apples. I closed my eyes, and a soft moan escaped my mouth.

"You need a man," Dominic remarked with a teasing smirk.

"I agree," Gina chimed in.

I chose to ignore them.

"You missed your calling," I told Dominic, trying

to redirect the conversation.

"I agree," Gina concurred. "Feel free to break into my house anytime to whip up breakfast. In fact, if you keep this up, I might give you a key."

"Good, because between the dead body in your backyard and the chaos of the car lodged in your living room, this place is the most exciting spot in town," he quipped, using his knife and fork to skillfully cut the turnover into perfectly bite-sized pieces. "So, how did last night go?"

We began our tale with the events of the fire and the tragic death at the nursing home. The story took a twist, culminating in the eerie incident of body snatching at the morgue.

"Wow, if I didn't know any better, I'd think you were lying," Dominic remarked, disbelief etched across his face. "Who would even think to steal a body?"

"That's the million-dollar question," Gina replied.

"Speaking of missing persons, where's Krista?" I inquired.

"She headed out early to change before her shift at work," Gina explained.

"I left my water bottle on the counter," Dominic said, attempting to rise.

"Hold on, let me grab it for you," Gina said with a burst of enthusiasm. She reached for her purse, perched on the table, and rummaged through it. Pulling out a gaming remote and her phone, she grinned, her eyes sparkling excitedly. "I've been wanting to try this out." She began to maneuver the joysticks, producing a clicking noise.

Dominic waited impatiently. "I'm going to wither away from thirst," he declared dramatically.

"Give me a moment. Rome wasn't built in a day," Gina replied.

The front door slowly opened as MARTI, the sleek robotic figure, emerged. Attached, just below his camera, was a sturdy metal hook from which a small pouch dangled. Inside the pouch was a water bottle. MARTI glided towards Dominic, his articulated claw expertly extracting the water bottle from the pouch and extending it forward.

"That's quite an impressive feat of engineering for a robot of this kind," Dominic observed. "What algorithms are you running?"

Gina and Dominic engaged in an intense discussion about robotics, their conversation filled with technical jargon that sounded much like the adult voice in a Charlie Brown cartoon. Gina had a mechanical engineering degree before entering the military, so it was no surprise that she was trained to run EOD robots.

I shoved the last bite of turnover into my mouth, then licked the icing off my fingers. Afterward, I reached into my pocket and retrieved the green thumb drive.

"Here's your ducky," I said, handing it to Domonic.

"I'll get right on it when I get home," he replied.

I had just picked up my second mouth-watering pastry when I heard the rumble of engines seconds before the sheriff's patrol car pulled into the driveway, closely followed by a black car.

"Here we go," I muttered, reluctantly setting the turnover back onto the plate.

Sherrif Earl stepped out of the car and slammed the door with such force that the sound caught Jean's attention across the street. She whipped her head around in surprise. In her distraction, she accidentally watered her shoe instead of the flower she was aiming for.

With an air of authority, Earl marched up the steps with heavy, purposeful strides, glaring at me.

"Well?" he growled.

I quickly shifted my gaze to Gina, who merely shrugged in response, her expression unreadable. I returned my eyes to the sheriff.

"Are you here for breakfast?" I inquired, lifting the plate of freshly baked pastries and extending it to him.

I caught a glimpse of a grin spreading across Blake's lips. He and Sean strolled up behind the sheriff, halting at the bottom of the porch.

The sheriff's mouth tightened into a grim line as he regarded me. "You know damn well why I'm here," he replied sharply. "You two disabled my vehicle and broke into the morgue last night."

"I don't recall that, but it sounds more exciting than spending another evening watching movies like we did last night," Gina quipped, a playful smirk dancing on her lips.

The sheriff remained stone-faced, his beady eyes boring into me, reminding me of the wretched chickens.

"Why would anyone want to break into a morgue?" I pondered. "Do they keep a lot of money there?"

Earl's face twisted in disbelief as he shouted back. "You went there to steal a dead body!"

"That's disgusting," Dominic said.

"Yes," I replied, my voice tinged with irritation as I rose to my feet. The sheriff's persistent mistreatment gnawed at me. "We stole the dead body to sacrifice it. We laid it in the backyard surrounded by candles, did our chanting, and drank goat blood."

"Can you sacrifice a dead body?" Dominic asked. "I thought it was only a sacrifice if the person was living."

"And it wasn't a full moon," Gina chimed in, her voice laced with mischief. "Us witches can only drink goat's blood during full moons. Everyone knows that."

Blake struggled to maintain his composure, the corners of his mouth twitching upwards as he fought to suppress a grin. Sean coughed into his hand to hide his laugh. A crimson flush started on the Sherrif's neck, slowly creeping up to his cheeks. Rage burned in his eyes.

"You think you're so smart," Earl said. He got up in my face and jabbed a pudgy finger into my chest. "One minor misstep from you, and not only am I throwing you in jail, I'm getting you drummed out of the military."

I went straight from irritated to mad as hell. My nails bit into my palms. It took every ounce of self-control I possessed not to lose my temper and break him in half.

"Any part of you that touches me, you're not getting back," I hissed through clenched teeth.

"Uh-oh," I heard Gina whisper to Dominic. "Call the paramedics."

Something in my expression must have conveyed the seriousness of the situation because Earl drew back his finger as if it had touched fire.

"Are you threatening me?" he snarled.

"That's a promise," I shot back defiantly. "Now, if you've got no evidence to arrest us, I suggest you leave this property."

He glared. "This isn't over." He stomped off the porch, barreling through Sean and Blake, who wisely stepped aside to avoid his descent.

"What do you two want?" I shouted at Sean and Blake, my frustration bubbling over as the sheriff whipped his car around with a screech of tires, tearing out of the driveway in a huff. Anger coursed through me, ready to erupt like a volcano, as I felt the urge to lash out at anyone nearby.

Dominic whistled, "I know not to make her mad."

Blake and Sean simultaneously raised their hands.

"We just need to ask Gina and you a few questions," Blake said, looking at me warily.

I closed my eyes and took a deep breath. "Sorry,"

I said sinking back down in the chair.

"Since the two of you were at the gravesite yesterday morning for the exhumation of the body, we need to ask where you were last night," Blake said.

Gina furrowed her brow in mock confusion. "Does this have something to do with the morgue break in the sheriff mentioned happening last night?"

"Did someone do something to Evaline's body?" I asked.

Sean glanced at Blake, who gave him a nod.

"Evaline's body was stolen last night."

"This town has become so weird since I left. How often do bodies get stolen around here?" I asked in all honesty because I was still confused about the body snatching last night.

"Are you accusing us of breaking into the morgue too?" Gina asked.

"Actually, no," Blake said, surprising me.

"A man was walking his dog last night and saw two people in a white minivan wearing ski masks pull into the back driveway of the funeral home. He thought it was odd, so he called the police. Sean told me Krista was with you two last night, so I can't imagine you doing it without her."

"Krista doesn't know anyone who owns a van," Sean said. "Besides, my wife would probably throw up if she saw a dead body."

It was close.

"If you don't think we stole the body, why are you asking us where we were?"

"Evidence suggests there may have been a second set of burglars," Blake said.

"Really," Gina replied. "There are some sick people in this town."

"What makes you think there were more people involved?" I asked.

Blake leaned forward. "The perps in the van broke into the morgue through the garage door, but the locked door leading to the funeral home was hanging wide open, and the side door was unlocked as well."

"Maybe the crew in the van went poking around the funeral home looking for more bodies," Gina suggested.

"I don't think there was enough time for that," Blake countered, his eyes narrowing with skepticism.

"Besides," Sean added, "It took Krista twenty minutes to respond to the text I sent last night."

Gina chuckled. "Well, we were rather wasted," Gina said. "There was a Legally Blonde marathon on last night."

Blake looked puzzled. "You got drunk watching Legally Blonde?"

I nodded, a grin creeping onto my face. "Every time someone said something stupid, we took a shot. And let me tell you, it happened a lot."

"What were you drinking?" Sean asked.

"White wine," Gina and I answered in unison.

Sean nodded. "That's Krista's favorite."

As Blake started to turn away, Dominic suddenly asked, "What happened to the sheriff's car?" I shot him a warning glance, hoping to avoid that topic.

"Last night, someone put his car up on blocks so it wouldn't move. When he got the call about the morgue break-in, he couldn't get out of his driveway to respond," Sean explained.

Dominic laughed.

"I wish I could have seen his face when he found out," I said, a smirk playing on my lips, not bothering to hide my amusement.

"I didn't see it last night either, but I was at his house this morning," Blake said, unable to suppress a smile. "It took Officer Connor thirty long minutes to get the car down while Earl barked orders."

It figured that the sheriff was too lazy to do the work himself.

"It was probably a group of teenagers pulling a prank," Gina suggested.

"I'm sure," Blake responded, sounding unconvinced.

They made their way to the car, and just as they closed the doors, Dominic's curiosity broke the stillness. "Did you really put the sheriff's car on blocks?"

"Bricks, to be precise," Gina responded, a smirk playing at the corners of her lips.

Dominic laughed, then pushed himself off the swing. "Now that the excitement is over for the morning, I think I'll head home and check out what's on this drive."

Chapter 14

It was early afternoon when the doorbell chimed. Gina was in the yard feeding the dog and chickens, which left me to respond to the unexpected visitor. As I opened the door, I was greeted by Mini.

"What are you doing here?" I inquired.

"During craft time, I whittled a bar of soap into a knife and overpowered the guards," she replied sarcastically. "It's an apartment building, not a prison. I drove here." She pushed past me into the house, stopped in the living room, and looked around the open space.

"Not much into decorating, is she?" Her gaze shifted to me. "I'm here to talk to you about Pearl."

That piqued my interest. "Please sit down," I invited, gesturing to the empty chair.

She shook her head. "I'm heading to the bowling alley. I just wanted to let you know... she was murdered."

I was surprised. "Why do you believe she was murdered?"

"Half an hour before she was found, she was in my apartment. We each had a shot of Tequila. Afterward, she left to head back to her place. She was healthy as a horse and in good spirits when she left. The sudden news of her death hit me like a freight train." She sighed. "She was my best friend, and I want her killer brought to justice. I need you both to find out who did this."

"How close is her apartment to yours?" I asked.

"Directly across the hall," she replied.

"And you didn't hear anything out of the ordinary?"

"I distinctly heard a loud bang. I stepped into the hall to see what it was. I didn't hear anything further, so I returned to my apartment."

"How often did you and Pearl get together for drinks?"

"Every night. Pearl was a stickler for routine. Like clockwork, we would settle in for a few rounds of gin rummy and savor a drink or two before she would inevitably head home. She was disciplined about her schedule, promptly going to her bed by six-thirty each evening."

If all elderly people went to bed this early, it was no wonder the old ladies across the street were always up before dawn.

"Who all knew about this nightly routine?"

She paused for a moment, her brow furrowing in thought. "Everyone, I suppose," she finally answered.

That didn't help narrow down our suspect list.

"I really must go," she said, glancing at her watch. "My bowling partner will be wondering where I'm at. I'll keep an ear to the ground at home and let you know if I stumble upon anything interesting." With that, she began to make her way back to the door.

"One final question," I called out, and she paused, turning to face me. "Is it possible your husband went somewhere other than the gym every day? We checked the only gym in town, and he wasn't a member there."

She regarded me as if I had just suggested that a camel might have three heads, and she was questioning my sanity.

"Are you high?" she asked.

"What?" I replied, taken aback.

"He didn't go out to a gym. He used the gym

above the garage," she clarified.

Just then, Gina stepped into the room.

"You have a gym above your garage?" I directed at Gina.

She halted mid-stride, and with an audible thump, she banged her palm to her forehead. "Duh. I totally forgot about it."

"How on earth do you forget a whole room on your property?"

"I never use it," she replied.

I rolled my eyes. When I turned back around, Mini had already disappeared.

We made our way out the back door and headed towards the garage. Wilber bounded over to Gina, his tail wagging furiously, eager for her affection. As we strolled past Cagney, her glare felt like a sharp dagger aimed directly at me. She took two deliberate steps in my direction, her expression filled with menace.

In response, I lifted the back of my t-shirt, revealing the glint of my firearm that caught the sunlight, reflecting it like a warning beacon. It sent an unspoken message Cagney understood because she abruptly turned, sticking her butt in the air, and waddled back towards Lacey.

On the side of the garage was a rickety old wooden staircase leading up to a second-floor door. As I cautiously placed my foot on the third step, it creaked and groaned so loudly I thought it would break in two. I gripped the railing for support, succeeding in giving myself an oversized splinter that sent a sharp sting through my hand. I looked at my finger, and my eyes widened at the size of the splinter. It made a sewing needle look small. I yanked it out, and blood started to seep out of the site. I wiped my hand on my pants before carefully ascending the stairs while avoiding the railing.

At the top, I encountered a metal door that had

faded to a dull, peeling blue. Gina slid her key into the rusty lock with a soft click and swung the door open wide. I was surprised to see that what lay beyond wasn't just a room but a small apartment. Light poured in through the bare windows, illuminating the space without the need for artificial light. The living room and kitchen were separated by a counter bar, giving it a cozy feel. Two doorways led off the main room, but the sight of gym equipment captivated me. The main area was overtaken by a Bow flex, treadmill, and exercise bike.

The place had a musky, unused smell. Cobwebs hung in the corners of the ceiling, and dust was layered so thick on the treadmill belt that you could write your name on it.

"The only time I ventured up here was when I considered buying it. Mini had mentioned she would leave the equipment behind, but I never took the time to look."

We began our search in the kitchen. There were no appliances, but we opened cabinet doors and drawers to search through them. Inside, we found nothing but a single, dead mouse curled up in the corner. Neither Gina nor I was willing to touch it, so we shut the door and left it alone. There was nothing in the living room but the dusty exercise equipment, so we approached the first side door.

Behind it lay a bedroom, sparsely furnished with a bed covered in a thick layer of dust. I lifted the top mattress, hoping to uncover a hidden secret, but it revealed nothing. As I set it back down, a cloud of particles erupted into the stagnant air.

Between the two rooms was a cramped bathroom, and we quickly cleared it of any secrets before making our way to the smaller of the two bedrooms. In the corner sat several boxes, haphazardly piled and pushing against each other. We sifted through them but only found old baseball trophies and memorabilia.

"Nothing," I sighed as I started emptying the last box.

"What were we hoping to find?"

"Something," I exclaimed, throwing my hands skyward in exasperation. "Anything. A clue that might explain why he spent so much time up here."

As I rummaged deeper into the boxes, I stumbled upon a faded photograph of Mini and Charlie. His midsection protruded so prominently that it made him look as if he were eight months pregnant. I held the picture up for Gina to see.

"Clearly, he didn't come here to exercise," I remarked, tossing the picture back into the box with a sense of finality.

We returned to the living room. I pressed the power button on the treadmill, and the control board flickered to life, ready for use. I hesitated for a moment before switching it off again.

"Maybe he hid it somewhere harder to find," Gina suggested.

"This is not a spy novel," I reminded her.

She crossed her arms. "If you had something important to hide, wouldn't you stash it behind a false wall or a disguised outlet cover?"

With a resigned sigh, I knelt beside an electrical outlet. I opened my pocket knife and turned it into a makeshift screwdriver, removing the tiny screw. As I pulled off the plate, a wave of disappointment washed over me; nothing but wires and dust lay behind it. I replaced the plate with a soft click and stood, about to move on, when I caught Gina gazing intently at the dome light overhead.

"What are you thinking?" I asked.

She pointed upwards. "One of the screws is halfway out. The light is large enough to conceal a file folder or something else of value. We need to remove the other two screws and look."

"We'll need a ladder."

"No, we won't," she replied confidently. "The light is directly above the seat of the bike. I'll stand on the seat and use your knife to take the screws out."

All sorts of horrible images flashed through my mind. Gina, balancing on a small bike seat wielding a knife in her hand, had disaster written all over it.

"Why don't I do it?" I suggested.

"Nonsense, I'm in the prime of my life. Now help me up."

With a sigh, I steadied her as she stepped onto the seat. To my surprise, she managed to find her balance, wobbling slightly but staying upright. I handed her my knife, watching as she placed one hand firmly against the ceiling for support while the other worked to remove the screws.

Everything was going smoothly until the second screw fell out and clattered to the ground, which sent the light fixture tumbling from its mount. It snagged on the remaining screw that hung half-in, causing it to swing down wildly. It flew back, hitting Gina in the face.

The impact knocked her off balance, causing her to drop the knife. She teetered and started to fall off the seat. On her way down, her legs kicked out, hitting the exercise bike's seat, knocking it over into the treadmill, the echo of metal against metal ringing in the air. I reached out to grab her and help lower her to the ground. I was unable to keep her upright, and we both toppled over, landing unceremoniously on our backsides next to the overturned bike.

The light fixture dangled from its screw for several more seconds until, with an abrupt snap, the screw finally yielded. It tumbled to the floor with a resounding crash. The inside of the light shade was noticeably vacant.

"Well, that wasn't worth it," Gina muttered.

"You think?"

I stood up and reached for the bike's handle to set it upright. As I began to lift it, a sudden pop echoed through the air, followed by the unmistakable sound of something else clattering against the floor.

"What was that?" I asked.

"The wheel cover came off," Gina remarked from her seated position.

I circled the bike with the intent on reattaching the cover. As I bent down, I saw a green spiral notebook lying on the floor beside it. I glanced into the hollow cavity of the bike and noticed the absence of a belt or flywheel. Instead, I found a plain wooden box with a shiny padlock glimmering in the dim light.

"Bingo," Gina explained excitedly. She picked up the notebook and opened it.

Her brow furrowed. "I don't understand any of this." She flipped through several pages. "It's written in some kind of code."

She handed me the notebook, and I quickly skimmed through the mysterious contents before tossing it aside. My eyes were drawn back to the box, and I carefully pulled it out. Reaching into my boot, I retrieved my lock picks and went to work on the lock.

"I'm starting to see why you always carry those with you," Gina commented.

With a click, the lock surrendered, and I lifted the lid, revealing a collection of shiny metal objects within. I withdrew one and examined it closely. It was about a foot long, shaped like a stake, with a round metal ball perched at an angle on top. Six of these bizarre objects were in the box.

"What is that?" Gina asked.

"I have no idea."

Just then, the step outside creaked. I peered

through the doorway, spotting a shadow creeping up the stairs. I pulled my gun, steadying my aim and bracing for the arrival of our uninvited visitor.

Suddenly, Dominic came into view.

"Gina girl, you've got to do something about these stairs," he exclaimed. His gaze darted to my gun, and he quickly dodged to the left, pressing himself against the wall.

"What are you doing here?" I asked as I lowered my weapon.

"Is it safe to come in?" He peered cautiously through the doorway. When he saw that it was clear, he stepped inside. "I wanted to give you an update on my findings." He leaned against the kitchen counter. "Over the past year, there have been fifty-four deaths at Meadow Springs."

"That seems unusually high," Gina remarked.

Dominic nodded. "The two years prior, there were about forty-eight deaths each year, but four years ago, there were only fourteen deaths.

"That's a drastic difference," I said.

"So, what changed?" Gina asked.

"That's the unknown question," he replied. "I reviewed the health records of each person who died this year. Thirteen were terminally ill, and another two were on a downhill spiral, likely heading for a nursing home."

"That only accounts for fifteen," I noted, eyebrows raised. "What about the rest?"

"That's just it," he said. "All of them had some underlying health issues, but nothing that should have led to death. Sure, heart attacks happen now and then, but a number this high of unaccountable deaths raises a lot of red flags."

"And everyone was deemed to have died of natural causes?" I asked.

Dominic nodded. "The death certificates were

very generic: old age, heart attack, the normal stuff."

"And no one questioned this uptick of deaths in the facility?" Gina asked.

Dominic shrugged. "I guess when your family member is old and living in a senior home when you are told they died of a legitimate reason, you accept it."

"What about the staffing during the deaths?" I inquired.

Dominic reached into the pocket of his black silk shirt and pulled out a folded piece of paper. "Two nurses were present during nearly all of the unaccountable deaths," he revealed, his expression shifting as he glanced at the note in his hand. "A Shirley Stahl and Bridget Coons."

Gina leaned closer. "So, either one could be involved or both."

Dominic nodded. "I'll dig deeper into their backgrounds and scan their social media accounts. There must be some incriminating evidence out there."

"Why kill a bunch of elderly people?" Gina pondered aloud. "And steal their bones?"

Dominic pushed off the counter and looked into the mysterious box beside me. "What are those?"

"We don't know," I replied. "I figured I'd do some web surfing and see if I could figure it out."

Dominic nodded and bent down to pick up the discarded notebook. As he flipped through the pages, his eyes danced with excitement. "This is written in code," he said.

"Yeah, and we're never going to figure it out," Gina said.

"I love decoding things. Can I take a crack at it?" he asked eagerly.

"Be my guest," I replied. He gleefully headed out of the room with a skip in his step.

* * * *

I ate a sandwich while I sat at the kitchen table. I scrolled through the search results, hoping to find some insight into the curious objects in the box beside me. Frustration rose as I picked one up, feeling the cold metal against my fingertips. I rotated it methodically, examining its surface, trying to decipher its purpose.

Gina strolled into the kitchen. She grabbed one of the objects from the box, her brow furrowing slightly as she inspected it.

"Have you figured out what it is?"

"Not yet," I replied, still turning the smooth piece of metal in my hands. As my thumb grazed a rough spot along the shaft, I paused and investigated it. "There's a number on here."

Gina leaned closer, her eyes glancing over the object in my palm. She rotated hers to examine the same area. "This one has a number too."

"Is it the same number?"

"No different," she replied after peering over my shoulder at the digits etched into the metal.

We pulled out several more from the box, each revealing a number as if they were all part of a mysterious code.

"They all have a number. Type one into Google and see if anything pops up.

I typed the digits into the search bar, but nothing concrete came up. I texted Dominic, and it only took a moment for my phone to ding in response.

"Across the street. Be over shortly," Dominic had texted.

As Gina tossed the object in her hand back into the box, the metallic clang echoed in the kitchen. "I think they're some type of tent stakes," she proposed.

"Really?"

"Sure, look at how it gets thinner beneath the ball area and widens at the top of the stake. That's where the tent strap would go."

The front door slammed shut, and Dominic strode in.

"That was quick," I remarked.

"Some people shouldn't own computers," he huffed. "Jean couldn't get hers to work, so she called me. And guess what? It wasn't even plugged in. I told her to box it up and return it to the store. So, what's going on here?"

"These weird stakes have numbers, but we can't figure out why," I explained.

"I don't think stakes are numbered. Let me take a look," he replied, taking my place in front of the computer.

As I paced the room, my mind wandered to darker thoughts. Why was Charlie killed? The notion that these objects were hidden gnawed at me. I didn't think that it was a coincidence, and I would bet on the fact that they were integral in his death. I walked over to the screen door, peering into the yard where Wilbur galloped around in blissful abandonment. The chickens lounged lazily under the oak tree, seeking refuge from the sun. Wilbur bounded over to them, planting his paws on the ground and coming to a halt before flopping down next to the chickens and resting his head on Cagney's back.

A memory flickered through my mind. The chaotic morning when they fought over a bone. If it hadn't been for their relentless digging, we never would have discovered the body hidden under the coop, and the investigation into Charlie's death would never have begun. Frustrated, I felt the urge to bang my head against the wall when a thought hit me like a bolt of lightning.

"What if those are some type of medical device?"

I blurted out.

"Like what?" Dominic asked, looking intrigued.

"Like an instrument used in surgery or something that would be implanted into a person. I used to work with a guy who was in a bad car accident and broke his arm. They put a metal rod in to stabilize it."

"I can try." Dominic started clicking away at the keyboard again.

Suddenly, the front door slammed open, and Krista stormed into the kitchen.

"Mini was in an accident," she blurted in a huff.

"What happened?" Gina asked.

Krista leaned against the back of the chair, taking a couple of deep breaths. She raised a finger to indicate she needed just a moment to catch her breath.

I glanced between Gina and Krista. "That's it. I'm putting you both on an exercise routine."

Krista rolled her eyes with dramatic flair, while Gina placed her finger under her chin and gave me a not-so-nice Italian gesture.

"Mini fell down the stairs at the apartment," Krista finally managed to say once her breathing steadied.

"Is she going to be okay?" I asked.

"I don't know," Krista said. "She was rushed to the hospital. When I showed up the nurse told me she was in surgery and wouldn't be out for several hours."

"What a coincidence that she was here only a few hours ago, and now she had a terrible accident," Gina remarked, her tone laced with skepticism.

"I don't believe in coincidence. I'd bet money that this was no accident," I said.

Gina's phone rang, and she grabbed it off the table. "Hell... uh-huh...but... I understand," she said. She tossed the phone back onto the table with enough force to create a loud thud. "We just got fired."

"What do you mean?" I asked.

"That was Thomas York. We've been officially removed from the case. He no longer wants to investigate the deaths at Meadow Springs. He thinks our presence has only caused more trouble."

The room fell silent as we stared at Gina.

"What?" she finally asked.

"You blew up a trash can," I pointed out.

"And started a fire," Krista added.

"Picky, picky," Gina replied.

"I found out what these are," Dominic interjected, gesturing toward the open box. "They are the parts used for hip replacements." He picked one up, holding the spherical ball in his hand. "The ball fits into the hip bone like this," he said, wrapping his fingers around the ball. "The long pointy end goes down inside the leg bone."

Gina turned towards me. "What made you think this could be a medical device?"

"We have two cases. One with a dead coroner and another where people are dying from questionable means and bones are being removed from them. So, I thought, no one knows more about bones than a doctor, and a doctor would be the perfect person to remove one."

"And the coroner is a doctor," Krista added.

"The sutures on the corpse did look like they were done professionally."

"So, you think the two cases are connected?" Dominic inquired.

"Absolutely. What if Charlie was involved in the deaths at Meadow Springs? For some unknown reason he keeps a cryptic record of it in a notebook," I said, glancing at Dominic.

"I haven't had a chance to examine it yet."

I pressed on, my mind racing with possibilities. "What if Charlie wanted out of whatever he was involved in, and the other party decided to silence him?"

"Then they'd bribe the new coroner to cover their

tracks," Dominic added.

"That's plausible," Krista said. "Now we need to determine if Ben is in on this and who he might be collaborating with."

Gina clapped her hands enthusiastically. "Time for a stakeout."

"I'm going to stay here and run the numbers on these hip implants. See what I can uncover."

"Krista, can we borrow your vehicle?" Gina asked.

"Why do you need my car?" she replied.

"A bright yellow Mustang is impossible to miss. If we're tailing him, he'll spot us from a mile away," I said.

"Alright," Krista relented, "but only if Gina drives."

I place my hand over my heart as if offended. "Really?"

"I've seen your driving skills. She's the better choice between the two of you," Krista replied. "You can always take Dominic's car."

"No one touches my Porsche but me," he said.

"Grab some water from the fridge," Gina said. "Looks like it's just you and me on this mission."

Chapter 15

The coroner's office was on the second floor of the courthouse, its windows overlooking the rear parking lot. As Gina pulled into the lot, I saw a secluded corner space next to a nondescript white van, an ideal spot for conducting discreet surveillance. However, Gina veered sharply into the space beside Ben's Lincoln. In her haste, she misjudged the distance, clipping the passenger-side mirror with a loud crack that shattered the glass, sending glittering shards tumbling to the asphalt below.

"Oops," she muttered, her expression more amused than contrite.

"What are you doing?" I asked.

"I wanted to park close so we could break into his car without anyone seeing us," she replied, a mischievous glint in her eye.

"Well, you definitely succeeded in parking close enough," I said wryly. "But don't you think attempting to break into a car in broad daylight at a public location might be a rather reckless idea?"

Gina mulled it over for a moment. "Maybe you're right."

I couldn't help but wonder how Gina avoided being arrested before I arrived in town. "Move before someone sees you."

Gina shifted the gears and maneuvered out of her spot, backing into the vacant space beside the nearby white van.

"Do you know what time Ben gets off work?"

Gina shook her head. "I'm not sure. But the building closes at five."

I stole a glance at the clock on the dashboard. We still had over two hours to kill. I sank deeper into the plush seat, trying to make myself comfortable.

Less than twenty minutes had passed when Ben suddenly emerged from the building. He urgently hopped into his car, starting to back out when he abruptly hit the brakes.

He hopped out of the vehicle and hurried alongside it, pausing next to the shattered mirror that dangled from the frame. His eyes flicked to the shards scattered on the ground, and then he began scanning the parking lot warily.

"Duck," I said.

We both huddled low in our seats and didn't glance up again until we heard his car crunching over the gravel on the asphalt. Once he left the parking lot, Gina flicked on the ignition and followed him. I had to credit her for staying close enough to keep him in sight yet far enough back to remain undetected.

Our pursuit carried us several miles out of town until we reached a secluded gravel parking lot at the base of the Appalachian Mountain. Ben guided his Lincoln into the lot, parking it beside an old, rusted truck that appeared to have been forgotten by time. Grass grew halfway up the hubcaps, indicating that the truck hadn't moved in ages. Gina continued onward. Once the parking lot was out of view, she pulled alongside a large bush, which helped camouflage the vehicle.

"We're in the national park," Gina said. "He's in the parking lot for the hiking trails."

"Ben doesn't look like the athletic type to me," I remarked.

We exited the car and made our way through the dense woods. We reached the edge of the parking lot, where we crouched behind a large boulder.

"What do you think he's up to?" I inquired, peering through the trees.

Ben was sitting in the car with the windows down. Rock music pulsed from the car's speakers.

"Maybe he's waiting for someone," Gina suggested.

We huddled behind the boulder for over fifteen minutes. Finally, the strain overwhelmed Gina. "I have to sit before my legs give out," she murmured, plopping down on her butt with a soft thud.

"I need to get a closer look."

Before Gina could respond, I slipped silently into the shadows of the trees, making my way around the edge of the parking lot towards the rusting truck. I moved with purpose, gliding to the back of the vehicle.

Peering through the truck's shattered back window, I spotted Ben drumming his fingers restlessly on the steering wheel, the steady beat synchronizing with the music.

His gaze flickered to his wristwatch; impatience written across his features. Finally, he turned off the music and picked up his phone. I couldn't decipher whether he was texting it or making a call.

I glanced at the missing mirror, an opportunity presenting itself. If I was careful, I could slip along the side of the car undetected. Unfortunately, in the absent music, there was no way he wouldn't hear my boots crunching over the gravel. With a swift decision, I unlaced my boots and removed them, my stockinged feet now vulnerable against the coarse ground. I hurried over the gravel, tiny stones biting into my feet, but I ignored the discomfort and slid beneath the open window.

Ben was on the phone, his tone telling me he

wasn't happy.

"What do you mean you aren't coming? We need to talk." He held the phone tight to his ear, pausing as the other person shouted back. "And you said this was foolproof," he sighed. "If we don't meet and talk, I'm walking." Another pause. "Fine, I'll meet you at Tequila Tavern at eight."

I heard the phone slide across the leather seat beside him, landing with a soft thud when he threw it. I quickly moved back around the truck, retrieving my boots. I barely reached the tree line when the car suddenly backed up with a rapid screech. I ducked behind a tree as it halted, then it shot forward out of the parking lot, dust flying in all directions.

I found Gina sitting in the car, her impatience palpable as she waited for me. "What did you find out?" she asked.

As I fastened my seatbelt, I relayed the details of the conversation I overhead.

"Never heard of the place," she replied

"Let's head back to the house where we can look up the address," I suggested. "But first can we grab something to eat? I'm famished." We made a quick detour through a fast-food drive-thru on our way home.

"The passenger mirror being broken worked out for you," Gina smirked as we pulled into the driveway.

"I wouldn't go that far," I replied as I shut the door.

"Admit it. Me breaking that mirror was crucial for your little eavesdrop."

"Whatever"

When we entered the kitchen, Dominic was still glued to his spot at the table, his eyes focused on the laptop.

"Have you found anything?" I asked, depositing the food bags on the table.

Dominic eagerly opened a bag and pulled out a steaming burger. "Boy, have I got news for you. Those numbers on the side of the hip replacement parts are serial numbers. Every artificial body part, from joints to pacemakers, have their own unique serial number," he explained.

"Why?" Gina asked, taking a seat.

Dominic delved into another bag, retrieving a carton of french fries. "They started it after nine-eleven as a method to identify a deceased person or a lost body part."

"There's a cheery thought," Gina said before taking a bite of her sandwich.

"And there's more. All those serial numbers are stored in a national archive. It took me a few moments, but I managed to hack into the site," Dominic added, pride evident in his voice.

A frantic scratching and cheerful barking erupted from the back screen door. Wilbur must have caught a whiff of the burgers. Gina grabbed a handful of fries. She flung the treats into the backyard, and chaos ensued as the dog and chickens collided in a flurry of feathers and fur, scrambling for the scattered morsels.

Lacey snagged a fry and dashed off triumphantly, only to be pursued by Cagney, who quickly snatched the prize right from Lacey's mouth. Lacey hesitated, her beady eyes watching the retreating chicken for a moment before trotting across the yard to hunt for another fry.

"What did you find out about the ones we found?" I asked, popping a crispy fry into my mouth, savoring the salty crunch.

Dominic leaned forward, picked up a list of names from the table, and handed it to Gina. "These parts you found were registered to people who passed away in the last year Charlie was the coroner."

A look of disgust washed over Gina's face. "Oh

yuck, I touched a metal part that was inside a person." She dropped her burger back onto its wrapper and darted over to the sink. She scrubbed her hands vigorously under the water. After thoroughly drying them, she returned to the table.

Gina picked up Dominic's list and scanned the names. "I don't recognize any of these names."

"I didn't either," Dominic replied. "So, I did some snooping online. Four of the individuals died at home, and two lost their lives in car accidents. None were classified as suspicious."

"No surprise there," I said, leaning back in my chair.

Dominic continued. "Interestingly, three of the deceased home addresses were Meadow Springs."

"So, half of the dead are tied to the same facility we're investigating," Gina said.

Dominic held up four fingers. "One of the car accident victims was an employee at Meadow Springs. He worked as a housekeeper."

"Coincidence?" Gina inquired.

"As you know, I don't believe in coincidence," I said. "We need to head to that bar tonight and see who Ben's meeting. Maybe we can figure out what's going on."

"What bar?" Dominic asked.

I quickly filled him in on the phone conversation I had overheard.

A grin spread across Dominic's face. "You two are going to Tequila Tavern?"

"Yeah, why?" Gina asked.

His smile broadened, mischief sparkling in his eyes. "I don't think you'll fit in."

"Please tell me there isn't a dress code?" I interjected, my heart sinking at the thought.

Dominic's eyes twinkled with amusement. "No,

but you are not exactly the right clientele."

"I hope it's not a strip club," Gina said.

Dominic shook his head, his chest heaving as he stifled a fit of laughter, looking like he might burst at any moment.

"We haven't got all day. Out with it," I pressed.

"It's a drag club," Dominic announced. "Most women don't go in there. You two will stick out like sore thumbs."

A plan formed in my mind. "You're a guy, and Ben doesn't know you. You can go in and find out who he's meeting with," I suggested.

Dominic shook his head. "I don't mind going in, but I'm not going alone."

"Do you have a friend that can go with you?" I asked.

Dominic and Gina exchanged conspiratorial glances, their grins widening like two mischievous children.

"You," they declared in unison.

It quickly dawned on me what they were plotting, and I raised my hands defensively. "No. No way am I dressing up as a drag queen."

"It won't take much," Dominic insisted. "You're already a woman, so that's one obstacle we won't have to worry about. Some makeup and the right outfit are all you need."

"Don't forget a cool wig," Gina added, clapping her hands in delight as she embraced the idea.

"If you're so excited about it, why don't you do it," I offered.

Gina shook her head. "I need to stay outside to watch who goes in and out of the bar. I'll also be ready for a quick getaway if needed".

I dropped my head to my hands, exasperation creeping in. "Why do we always have to leave in a rush?

For once, can't we leisurely exit a place?"

"Besides," Gina continued ignoring my protest, "you're stealthier than I am."

That was true. If Gina went in, she'd likely spill a drink on Ben, knock over a candle, and set the entire place ablaze.

"Do I have to wear a dress?" I tentatively asked.

Dominic smile twisted into a smirk. "Well-"

"Forget it," I interrupted.

"Fine," Dominic replied with a sigh. "I'm sure I can find something other than a dress for you to wear." He crumbled his burger wrapper and threw it into the trash. Rising from his chair, he added, "I'm going to find you an outfit. I'll be back before you can change your mind."

That's what I was afraid of.

* * * *

Gina and I had retired to the living room to watch TV, or more appropriately, to take a nap since we had no idea how long our night would be. Just as I felt the weight of slumber pull me under, the shrill ring of Gina's cell phone jolted me awake, causing me to cringe. We had both chosen the same ringtone for my mother—a booming, theatrical voice of Darth Vader proclaiming, "The dark side is calling."

With a sigh, Gina rolled over on the sofa, her hand fumbling as she hit the speakerphone. I imagined she was still half asleep. Usually, when my mother called, she left it go straight to voicemail.

"Hello," Gina answered groggily.

"What have you exposed my daughter to?"

Instantly, Gina straightened, a look of shock washing over her face.

My mother continued without an answer. "I go

178

out of town for two days and return to my voicemail full of messages. First, there was a skeleton in your backyard, and now I hear you stole a body out of the cemetery. Are you out of your mind? Sydney is young and impressionable."

I chuckled softly. Before Gina could formulate a response, the front door flew open.

"Hi, girls," Krista's cheerful voice filled the room.

"Is that Krista?" my mom's voice cracked through the phone. "What's going on over there? Gina, I swear if you-"

"I'm sorry you have the wrong number," Gina interjected in a masculine voice before abruptly hanging up the call.

"Wow, Mom's on a rampage," Krista remarked, half-amused.

The phone rang again, but this time Gina, clearly wiser, let it ring.

"So where are we in the investigation?" Krista asked.

Gina quickly filled her in on our stakeout of Ben and tonight's trip to the club.

"You in drag." Krista laughed out loud. "I can't wait to see this."

No more than the words left her mouth, then Dominic strode through the door, a white plastic clothing bag clutched in one hand and two shoeboxes in the other. Genesis closely trailed him.

"What are you doing here?" I asked Genesis.

"She's my makeup expert," Dominic declared. "If anyone can transform you into a drag queen, it's her."

Reluctantly, I ascended the stairs, the weight of dread settling heavily on my shoulders. Sitting on my bed, I became the canvas as Genesis began layering my face with what felt like a gallon of thick, creamy foundation. The application process seemed to stretch for hours as she applied makeup to my eyelids and cheeks.

Dominic and Krista sat on the edge of my bed, their excitement palpable. Dominic leaned in as he gave me pointers on how to act like a drag queen.

"First and foremost, you are a lady and must act like one," he instructed.

Krista let out a snort. "You may need to be more specific. Sydney doesn't like to act like a lady."

She was right; I could hardly fault her for stating the obvious. The idea of dressing up excessively to attract a man was foreign to me. I had often watched other girls flutter their lashes and laugh at everything a guy said, all in a desperate bid for attention. The thought of becoming like that made my skin crawl.

"You know, act feminine," Dominic continued.

I gave him a blank stare.

"Really?" In an exaggerated display, he hopped off the bed. "First, you need to learn how to walk."

"I walk," I shot back.

"Not like a lady," he rebutted, standing on his toes as if he were balancing in high heels. He demonstrated, walking with one leg gracefully in front of the other, his movements fluid as he made his backside sway with each step. "This is called sashaying."

"She's never going to learn that in an hour," Genesis protested, shaking her head. "Keep it simple and just cover the basics."

"Fine," Dominic huffed, flopping back down on the bed. "You must be confident."

"That I can do."

"Not just confident; you need to be the grandest person in the room," he instructed. "Every so often, run your tongue over your teeth or lips." He demonstrated, slowly running his tongue over his lips, drawing attention to the delicateness of the gesture. "And when you run into another queen, you address her as sister."

"Now for the finishing touches," Genesis interjected. She opened a glitzy case that revealed what resembled two giant spiders.

"What are those?" I asked, my curiosity mingling with dread.

"Eyelashes," she replied.

I leaned back. "And you think you're putting those on me?"

"Of course she is. All the impersonators wear fake lashes," Dominic stated as if it were the most obvious thing in the world.

Genesis applied what looked like superglue to the back of the lashes, then carefully affixed them to my upper lids, holding them in place momentarily before removing her hand. They made my eyelashes feel four pounds heavier.

"Voila," she declared triumphantly.

"You look great," Dominic said.

Genesis then pulled from her bag a flesh-colored orb that resembled a deflated kickball.

I arched my brow in confusion.

"It's a bald cap. We need it to hide your hair," she explained.

"Why?"

"We can't have any of your hair slipping out from under the wig. It'll blow your cover," Dominic said.

Defeated, I exhaled heavily as Genesis meticulously tucked my hair under the cap, securing it with more adhesive.

"I'm going to need a drink after this," I muttered.

Krista pulled a bottle of whiskey from her purse. "I've got you covered."

My spirits briefly lifted. Once the cap was in place, I reluctantly hopped off the bed and went to the bathroom, dreading the moment I would face my reflection. As I caught a glimpse in the mirror, I practically jumped out of my skin, shock coursing through my veins. "Who the heck is that?" I thought.

My skin appeared a shade darker than usual, glowing under the light. My eyelids were adorned with royal blue eyeshadow that boldly swept all the way up to a thickly penciled brow. Dark red lipstick accentuated my lips, and the new lashes tickled my cheeks every time I closed my eyes.

When I returned to the bedroom, I froze in my tracks. Dominic stood there, holding a one-piece bodysuit that shimmered ominously under the lightning. It was covered in electric blue feathers cascading like a peacock's plumage

"I borrowed this from my friend Paxton." Dominic said.

The look of horror on my face was evident.

"You said no dresses." Dominic reminded me, a hint of amusement dancing in his eyes.

Just as I was about to protest, Krista held up what looked like oversized silicone breast. They were massive, easily a double D.

"It's a breastplate," Genesis said.

"If you tell me all queens wear them, I'm going to punch you in the nose."

Dominic put his hands on his hips. "Well, they do."

"I already have breasts," I protested, crossing my arms defensively.

"Yes, but not the size that make men stop and stare," Dominic stated.

At that moment, Krista passed me the bottle of whisky. I unscrewed the cap and took a generous, long swallow.

"Let's get this over with," I muttered, returning the bottle to her. "And keep that where I can reach it."

As the silicone slid coldly against my skin, its slick texture was jarring. It crept halfway up my neck like an invasive vine. It fit like a half-shirt. Just as we managed to secure it in place, Gina strolled in. Her eyes widened in disbelief, and then, without warning, she erupted into laughter.

After several moments, I finally asked, "Are you quite finished?"

She snorted, wiping a tear from the corner of her eye. "Jump up and down. I want to see them jiggle."

I gave her the finger.

I quickly slipped into the shimmering feather bodysuit, the soft plumes swirling around me as I moved. Genesis pulled out a matching blue wig, the hair swept up on top of the head and cascading down like a genie.

Dominic rummaged through the shoeboxes, revealing two pairs of royal blue shoes. One pair boasted fierce five-inch spiked heels, while the other offered a more grounded two-inch platform heel, ideal for balance. I opted for the second pair.

"I told you I could persuade her to wear heels," Dominic remarked triumphantly, directing a teasing glance at Krista. She frowned in annoyance, slapping a crumpled five-dollar bill into his open palm.

I fiddled at the exposed silicone around my neck. "Won't this be noticeable?"

"Don't worry, I've got that covered." Genesis dug into her makeup kit and pulled out a black lace choker. With a deft movement, she clasped it around my neck and declared, "Done. You look perfect."

They urged me to look at myself in the mirror, but I refused. It would probably give me nightmares for weeks to come.

"And if any of you even think of taking a picture, I'll kill you where you stand," I added.

"My work here is done," Genesis declared,

packing away her makeup kit as she prepared to leave.

"I'm heading home tonight to keep Sean from getting suspicious," Krista replied. "Make sure to call me when your home."

I adjusted my cleavage for the last time. "Let's get this over with," I said, a mix of determination and dread lacing my tone.

Chapter 16

Near the edge of town, we stepped in front of a nondescript brown building with a sign reading, "Tequila Tavern," in bold black letters illuminated by backlight.

"I thought it would look different," I remarked, peering skeptically at the unassuming facade.

"What did you expect? A neon sign flickering with rainbow letters?" Dominic shot back.

"Well, yeah," I admitted.

"The LGBT community values its privacy, too," Dominic responded. "That's probably why the person wanted to meet Ben here. It's a quiet part of town. Even if someone inside recognizes them, they're unlikely to spill the beans. It would break the unspoken code."

"After you get out, I'll pull across the street," Gina said.

The bouncer barely acknowledged us as we walked past him. Given my attire, I felt a prick of apprehension, but it seemed I blended into the eclectic atmosphere more than I had anticipated.

Stepping inside, I was surprised to find the interior reminiscent of many bars I'd visited. A stage occupied the rear of the room, extending out toward the center of the floor. Tables and chairs were scattered around the stage.

On the far side, away from the stage's lighting, booths were tucked away in the dim corners. This was a much more secluded area, perfect for whispered conversations.

"They will probably meet at one of the booths," I remarked, glancing around the venue.

Dominic nodded in agreement. "Let's grab a drink at the bar to blend in with the crowd."

I received no more than a few passing glances as I idled up to the bar.

The clientele consisted of men, punctuated by the presence of a dozen flamboyant drag queens. I spotted a striking Marilyn Monroe, a Cher, and a Tina Turner, each commanding attention in their own right. However, one performer towered above the rest—draped in a dazzling, sequined red dress that clung to her figure. Her matching red headpiece added another seven inches to her height, making her an unforgettable figure amid the crowd.

Dominic waved at the bartender, catching his attention.

"D man, what can I get for you?" the bartender asked with a friendly grin.

"Two Pina Colada's," Dominic responded. We had already discussed the drink selections most suitable for my undercover role. No beer or strong liquor for me.

As the bartender turned to prepare our drinks, I raised an eyebrow at Dominic.

"I may have been here once or twice," he replied.

As we leaned against the bar and waited for Ben to arrive, the queen in the red dress approached us. She looked elegant and moved as if floating on air. All eyes in the room were magnetically drawn to her, and I began to appreciate the captivating presence that defined a true queen.

Dominic introduced us. "Sydney, this is Paxton. The one I borrowed your outfit from."

"You can call me Starlight," Paxton said.

I struck a pose, placing one hand on my hip while

the other rested dramatically at my side, my wrist arched with exaggerated flair. In my best attempt at a drag queen accent, I exclaimed, "Sister, it is so nice to meet you!"

Paxton and Dominic exchanged bewildered glances.

"Too much?" I asked.

They both nodded, their faces lit up with amusement.

"Girl, you need to let your feminine side show. Don't try so hard," Starlight said, flicking her hair over her shoulder. "Got to go. I have a hot prospect on the line."

As Starlight sauntered away, I caught sight of Ben entering the bar. He moved purposefully toward a shadowy corner booth, his gaze sweeping across the crowded room, scanning for a familiar face. I quickly averted my eyes as he searched.

Moments later, Marilyn approached him. They exchanged a few hushed words before she turned, strutted toward the bar, and paused beside me.

"Reno, I need a whiskey on the rocks," she yelled to the bartender.

This was my chance. I gently tapped her on the shoulder. She spun around, her expression shifting from annoyance to surprise as our eyes locked.

"Do you mind if I take that gentleman his drink?" I asked.

"Bitch, you trying to steel my tip?"

"No, I just want to talk to him." I shifted uneasily in my skin-tight bodysuit, acutely aware of the absence of pockets to conceal my money or even the gun I usually carried. I wasn't happy about the latter, but Dominic assured me he had me covered.

With a quick jab of my elbow into Dominic's side, he responded by retrieving his wallet and producing a twenty-dollar bill, which he casually handed over to

Marilyn. "This should more than cover the tip," he said.

Marilyn gave me a skeptical once-over, her gaze lingering on the contours of my figure. "Suit yourself," she replied, arching an eyebrow. "But take my advice. You're way too good for the likes of him."

I grabbed Ben's drink and strolled across the bar. The atmosphere was thick with distant music and a mix of laughter, but my focus was solely on the table where Ben sat.

His glowing phone screen utterly absorbed him. I placed the glass down with a soft clink, hoping to grab his attention. "That'll be four dollars," I said, having no clue about the actual cost of the drink.

Without looking up, he slapped a five-dollar bill onto the table. "Keep the change."

I picked up the bill and was going to tuck it away, only to remember I had nowhere to put it. Because of the fake boobs, I wasn't even wearing a bra.

"Do you come here often?" I asked with a smile.

He finally lifted his gaze from the phone, and instantly, his attention was drawn to my overly ample cleavage. His eyes widened before he tore them away. "I'm meeting someone."

The crowd erupted into cheers and applause as the lights above the stage flickered on. Dolly Parton stepped onto the stage, her presence commanding the room. Men hooted and hollered, and I leaned over the table to bridge the distance.

"I can keep you company until they show up," I offered, making my way to the opposite side of the booth.

I glanced up as Dolly began to sing. I was surprised at the size of her boobs. They were huge, size G if such a size even exists. They made my new double D's look small in comparison.

Ben shot me a dismissive look. "I'm not interested. Move on," he replied, his tone leaving no room for negotiation.

At that moment, a loud bang erupted inside the bar, resembling the sound of a gunshot. Ben's eyes went wide, then rolled back into his head as a crimson stain started to spread across his chest. He slumped forward in the booth.

Dolly must have caught sight of the scene before me, for she let out a piercing scream. Panic erupted as everyone in the room surged toward the exit. As I spun around, a flash of red light caught my eye to the left, and I noticed the emergency door slowly closing. I made a beeline for Dominic, urgency propelling me forward.

"Hand me your gun," I said.

He pulled a small taser out of his blazer pocket.

"This isn't a gun?" I shouted.

"I said I had a weapon. I didn't specify a gun."

"This barely qualifies as a weapon!" I exclaimed, my voice rising with frustration.

My eyes scanned the area, searching for anything more substantial. They landed on a paring knife on the bar beside a half-cut lemon.

I seized the knife and sprinted toward the emergency exit, the cool metal feeling solid in my grip.

I flung the door open and then halted, surveying the area. I was peering into a narrow alley between two buildings. At the far end of the alley, a rusted chain-link fence stood with a garbage dumpster wedged against it. The other end of the alley opened to the main street.

There were two options. Either the killer fled onto the main street and blended into the crowd, making it unlikely I would ever catch him, or he used the dumpster as a boost to scale the eight-foot fence. Suddenly, I heard a clanking echo behind the building, reminiscent of a metal can carelessly being kicked as someone fled.

I clambered onto the dumpster lid, which groaned in protest beneath my weight. I kicked off my heels, letting them hit the pavement, and grasped the top of the fence, preparing to pull myself up. As I began my ascent, a blinding white light flooded the alley.

"Freeze, Police!" a voice called out from behind me.

Crap.

I slowly raised my hands above my head and turned to face the blinding light that pierced the darkness. I was able to make out two silhouettes, their weapons aimed squarely at my chest.

"Get down from the dumpster," one of them commanded.

In one fluid motion, I jumped down, my arms still lifted in surrender, the knife in one hand.

"Drop your weapon."

I tossed the knife forward, and it thudded to the ground a couple of feet in front of me. At that moment, the officers began to advance cautiously. I squinted against the bright light as it zoomed in on me.

"Sydney, is that you?" asked the officer holding the flashlight as he lowered the beam to the ground.

Without the light shining in my face, I could get a good look at the two officers. Sean was the one holding the flashlight. Unfortunately, the other officer was Blake, his expression inscrutable, but his jaw hardened with tension.

Double crap.

"How did the two of you get here so quickly?" I asked.

"We were playing poker at a friend's house across the street when the call came in." As Sean's eyes roamed over me, a grin spread across his face, quickly transforming into a full-blown smile, stretching from ear to ear. His gaze lingered on my chest, and I could sense his amusement. "I don't remember you being this busty."

Sean jabbed his finger right into the middle of my

chest. The silicone felt oddly soft and squished under his touch, producing a comical sound that echoed in the silence. As he withdrew his finger, an amusing little dent remained.

Sean erupted into laughter and turned to Blake, gesturing dramatically in my direction. Through fits of laughter, he managed to choke out, "I can't... just can't." With that, he sauntered away, his hearty chuckles trailing behind him.

Blake, on the other hand, did not share in the amusement. His expression was stern and unyielding as he cast a quick glance at the knife at his feet before fixing me with a piercing glare.

"I know Gina is somewhere close by," he said, his voice steady and authoritative. "Grab her and whoever else is in your crew, then meet me inside." With that, he turned sharply on his heel and strode purposefully back down the aisle.

I reluctantly slipped the heels back on and crossed the street. Gina was still in her car. A scattering of people had rushed outside from the bar, but most had already fled, caught in confusion and fear. The wail of police sirens pierced the air, growing louder as several squad cars rocketed down the road, their lights flashing in a frantic display of red and blue.

As I approached Gina's car, she rolled down her window, her expression a mix of concern and urgency. "What happened in there?" she asked. "People ran out as if they accidentally stumbled into a political rally."

"Someone popped Ben."

Her eyes grew wide. "Did you see the shooter?"

"No, I was facing Ben at the time," I replied, the memory of the chaos still fresh in my mind. "The shooter ran out the emergency exit. Did you notice anyone exiting the alley?"

Gina shook her head. "Now what?"

"Blake wants to talk to us inside."

Her mouth formed a surprised 'O' as realization dawned on her, and she rolled up the window before stepping out of the car.

As we waited for Blake, Gina, Dominic, and I settled onto wooden bar stools.

"Are we going to jail?" Dominic asked, looking apprehensive as he nervously fiddled with the hem of his shirt.

Gina and I shrugged. While we waited, a uniformed officer approached and methodically swabbed my hands with a damp cotton ball, searching for traces of gunpowder residue.

"Is that necessary?" Gina asked. "She didn't shoot anyone."

"Just doing my job," the officer replied.

Blake and Sean approached us, their expressions a mix of irritation and disbelief. They were clearly not pleased to find us in the aftermath of chaos.

"Your initial residue test came back negative," Sean stated, making an effort to look me in the eyes. He probably didn't want to look at my chest so he wouldn't succumb to fits of laughter again.

"And you were only wielding a knife," Blake added. "And in that outfit..." he paused, taking in my attire, "It doesn't look like there's anywhere to hide a gun. I presume you are not the shooter. So, tell me, what happened here tonight?"

I recounted my brief exchange with Ben, sharing the details of what I had witnessed during the shooting and the aftermath that culminated in me precariously standing on a dumpster.

Blake pinched the bridge of his nose, his eyes fluttering closed momentarily as if bracing himself for the weight of my words. "Let me get this straight." He opened his eyes, fixing me with a piercing glare. "You thought it was wise to chase down a killer carrying a firearm, armed only with a three-inch kitchen knife?"

I simply shrugged.

"Are you trying to get yourself killed? Because if you want to die, I want nothing more right now than to shoot you myself."

"I wasn't trying to catch the shooter. I just wanted to get close enough to see who it was." I admitted. But deep down, I knew that was a lie. In truth, if I had managed to catch up with the killer, I would have unleashed every ounce of my strength to take him down.

Blake threw his hands in the air. "And you think that's better. Gina, where were you during all of this?"

"I was in the car," she replied.

Blake's gaze shifted to Dominic.

"I was standing at the bar right where we are now," Dominic said.

"Where's Krista?" Sean asked apprehensively as it dawned on him that she wasn't present.

"At home," we all said in unison.

Sean let out a relieved sigh.

Blake leaned forward, his eyes narrowing with an intensity that made Dominic and Gina shift uncomfortably. "Now tell me why you're here. I mean the real reason, not some elaborate tale about needing a night out. It better be good because if I'm not convinced, you're all going to jail."

The three of us exchanged glances, silently debating how much to reveal.

"You." Blake pointed at me. "Lady Gaga in the bird outfit. I want to hear the story from you."

I had to quickly sift through my thoughts, choosing my words carefully—enough to satisfy his curiosity and keep us out of trouble, but not so much that it could land us behind bars. "We thought maybe Ben had some knowledge about Charlie's death," I finally stated.

"Why's that?" Blake pressed, leaning in closer.

I went on to explain our peculiar discovery at the house—the hidden hip replacements and their former owners. I purposely omitted our unsettling suspicions about Charlie's possible involvement in the demise of those who once possessed these devices.

"You think these medical devices are what led to Charlie's death?" Blake asked.

"Maybe," I replied. "It just strikes me as odd that he had them in his possession."

"We thought maybe he was selling them on the dark web," Dominic added.

Blake nodded. "And how does Ben fit into this theory?"

"We wanted to see if he had picked up where Charlie left off. Or if Charlie had a partner who might have approached Ben to get him involved," I explained.

"And you figured that dressing in drag was the best way to confront him?" Blake replied with a hint of disbelief.

"Well," Gina interjected hesitantly. "We did attempt to engage him in a straightforward conversation first, but then we overheard him yelling at someone on the phone."

I went into the details surrounding the phone conversation I had accidentally overheard, choosing to omit the location.

Blake's eyes narrowed while deep lines etched themselves across his furrowed brow. "Why didn't you come to me with this information before parading around dressed like a flamboyant peacock?" he exclaimed, his voice rising in agitation. "You two didn't just compromise this case; you've pulverized it."

Sean stood nearby, silently absorbing the exchange, his head shaking in disbelief at the unfolding drama. Just then, his phone chimed. He glanced at the screen, his expression turning serious. "The sheriff has just arrived," he announced.

I locked eyes with Blake, an uneasy feeling settling in my stomach. I was convinced that if the sheriff found us here, I wouldn't just be on thin ice—I'd surely end up behind bars.

He let out a heavy breath and shook his head. "Go out the emergency exit before I change my mind, but first thing tomorrow, I'll be over for that box."

We didn't need to be told twice. With a quick leap off our stools, we bolted for the exit. As I reached the front of the alley, I cautiously peered around the building, ensuring the coast was clear. I darted across the street towards Gina's car, praying that when the sheriff pulled up, he was too preoccupied to notice her vehicle. No one spoke until the Mustang pulled away from the curb.

"Why didn't you mention the code book to him?" Dominic asked from the backseat.

"Or about Evaline's missing bone?" Gina added.

"Before we hand over the code book, you need to decipher its meaning," I said to Dominic. "And I want to keep the cops from sniffing around the funeral home."

"Why's that?" Gina asked.

"Because tonight we're going back to the morgue," I replied, my mind racing. "I have a gut feeling that Meadow Springs and the funeral home are at the very core of this mystery. With Pearl passing just last night, it would be wise to start our search at the morgue."

"Smart move," Gina agreed. "Who knows? They might be removing something significant from her."

"But who will be doing it now that Ben is gone?" Dominic asked.

"My guess would be Rocco," I replied. "He's the mortician there, and let's just say he doesn't seem like the type to hesitate about cutting open a body, whether it's breathing or not."

"Alright," Gina said, as she pulled the Mustang into her driveway. "Go upstairs and change clothes. I'll gather some provisions."

"I'm also tackling this mountain of makeup," I said, glancing at my reflection in the passenger window.

"I'll head home and dive into the encrypted notebook," Dominic said.

I dashed up the stairs and peeled off the bodysuit. As I pulled it away, a flurry of blue feathers erupted like tiny confetti, swirling around me. The suit still looked full of feathers, but my bedroom looked like there was an explosion at a pillow factory, with feathers clinging to every surface.

I made my way to the sink, desperately scrubbing at my face, but the remnants of makeup stubbornly clung on. My fingers fumbled as I tried to pry off the false lashes, but they seemed to have fused with my eyelids. Frustrated, I leaped into the steaming shower, letting the hot mist envelop me, hoping it would loosen the stubborn glue. I spent a good ten minutes washing away the remnants of the night.

Once I emerged, I quickly changed and hurried out the door, ready to tackle the next challenge.

Chapter 17

It was close to midnight when we finally parked our car on the street outside the morgue, partially concealed by a cluster of bushes. From our vantage point, we had a good view of the back of the building. However, with no windows in the morgue, we were unable to tell if anyone was inside.

We sat in silence, and after several moments, Gina's impatience began to bubble to the surface. She started to rhythmically tap her thumbs on the steering wheel. Eventually, she began to hum along.

"What are you humming?" I asked.

"Theme song to 'The A-Team'."

"Never heard of it," I admitted.

"It was before your time." She lowered her hand from the steering wheel. "How long are we going to sit here, just waiting?"

"I don't know," I sighed. "I'm waiting to see if something happens."

"And if it doesn't?"

I thought about it. "We'll wait for a while. If nothing happens, we'll break in again."

Silence filled the car once more, but it didn't last long. Soon, the rhythmic sound of Gina tapping her nails on the center armrest broke through.

"Have you been enjoying your time since you've returned?" she asked.

"Are you kidding?" I replied with a wry smile. "Since I've been home, I've seen more dead people than a serial killer."

"I'm being serious," Gina insisted, her expression softening as she turned to face me.

I took a moment to contemplate her question. "It's kinda been fun," I admitted. "It makes me miss work."

"Oh," she responded, her tone revealing a tinge of disappointment.

"What?"

Gina traced her finger around on the armrest. "I was hoping that maybe you enjoyed being back enough to consider staying."

"I don't think so." Back when I left home, I was the typical teenager who wanted to get away from the life I had always known and find something new. At that time, I didn't know what I wanted to do; I only knew that I wanted to make a difference in the world. I enlisted in the army mainly because my grandfather and aunt were already serving. Never in my wildest dreams could I have imagined that my journey would lead me to this point. Being a CI agent filled me with an immense sense of pride and purpose as I realized that my actions contributed to making the world a safer place. I could never give that up.

My thoughts were cut short as a car pulled into the back driveway. A gray sedan turned around, backed up to the garage door, as the trunk popped open.

"Show time," Gina said.

A man leaped out of the driver's side of the car and approached the morgue. He knocked several times on the garage door. The garage door began to rise, halting a few feet above the ground. From the shadows beneath the door, a large red cooler with a white lid was maneuvered outward.

"What do you think is in the cooler?" Gina asked.

I shrugged.

The man hefted the cooler by its handles, his muscles straining as he lifted it into the trunk of the car before slamming the lid shut. Without sparing a moment, he dashed back into the vehicle.

"Follow that car," I instructed.

The car was about a block away when Gina turned on the engine, the headlights piercing through the night. We navigated through the quiet streets, the faint hum of the engine filling the air as we headed south through town.

"We need to see what's in that cooler?" I urged.

"I can tail him to his destination, then we can sneak a peek," Gina suggested.

I hesitated. "But what if he doesn't stop anytime soon? We don't have all night to follow him."

As we passed the intersection of Washington Street, my phone buzzed in my pocket. I fished it out and placed it on speaker.

"Hello."

"I just heard what happened to Ben. I can't believe it," Krista's voice cracked through the line.

"Sean called and told you?" Gina asked.

"No, he called to say they'd be working all night," Krista explained. "I swung by the station to drop off snacks and energy drinks for the guys, and one of the patrol officers filled me in on the details. So, what are you two up to?"

"Following a lead," I replied.

"He's making a turn onto Colonial," Gina announced. "It looks like he's heading for the highway."

"I'm on Colonial," Krista chimed in. "Getting ready to turn onto Fuller to head home."

"Hold on, don't turn yet," I said.

"Why?" Krista asked.

"We need to catch a glimpse of what's inside the

car we're tailing," I said, glancing over at Gina. "How far ahead of us is she?"

"A couple of miles," Gina replied.

"Perfect. Krista, pull over to the side of the road and pop your hood. Get out of your vehicle and stand in front of it."

"I get it," Gina replied. "The classic damsel in distress routine."

"Exactly."

I heard Krista's car door shut with a solid thud through the phone. "I'm in position," she called out.

"Once you see the headlights, wave your hands to flag him down," I said.

Gina kept a safe distance from the vehicle. As we crested the hill, the faint glow of Krista's blinking taillights flickered in the distance.

"Here we come. Get ready," I said.

"What's your plan once he pulls over?" Gina asked.

"I hadn't thought that far ahead," I admitted.

"So, we're winging it. I love it when we do that."

It scared me when we did that. Something always went wrong.

We were close enough to see Krista waving her arms frantically. The driver, however, showed no signs of slowing down, his vehicle roared past without even a flicker of brake lights.

"Of all the nerve!" Gina exclaimed. "What kind of creep drives by without stopping to help a stranded woman in the middle of the night?"

"In this case," I replied, "a smart one."

I heard the heavy thud of a car door slamming shut, followed by the roar of Krista's SUV starting up. "He just drove right past me! Now, what do I do?" she shouted, her voice laced with frustration.

I was out of ideas, my mind racing. "I don't know.

Once he hit the interstate, there's no telling where he's headed."

Gina's eyes gleamed with determination. "I have a rifle in the trunk."

"That doesn't do us any good while driving down the road."

"No, silly. Wait until he hits the on-ramp to the highway. I can pull over on the bridge, and you can shoot out one of his tires."

A broad smile creased my lips. "That may be the best idea you've ever had."

"That's absurd. I come up with plenty of great plans," Gina shot back.

"Sure, but most of them seem to end with someone getting injured or us fleeing for our lives."

"Nobody's perfect," she shrugged, the corners of her mouth twitching upward.

"Krista, I'll call you back," I said as I hung up.

Gina revved the engine and accelerated, inching us closer to the vehicle we were tailing. The highway sign loomed ahead, and the driver ahead flicked on his turn signal to head south.

Gina maneuvered the car to the side of the road, the tires crunching over the gravel with a rough sound. She parked abruptly, and without a second thought, we both flung open our doors and darted out as we made our way around the vehicle, ready to execute our plan. Inside the trunk was a rifle with a scope, a bulletproof vest, a baseball bat, a whip, and a canvas duffle bag that I didn't want to open. If I knew what was inside, I would never get in the car again.

"No knife?" I joked.

"I keep that under my driver's seat."

I shook my head, reached into the trunk, and retrieved the rifle. With a practiced motion, I pulled back the bolt and inspected the chamber.

"Do you always keep a loaded rifle in your trunk?" I asked.

"You never know when you might need it."

I just loved this woman.

Leaning over the bridge's guardrail, I peered down, the faint glow from the taillights casting flickering shadows on the pavement below. The light illuminated just enough to reveal the contours of the tires. Taking a deep breath, I steadied myself, aimed, and as the air slowly escaped my lungs, I squeezed the trigger. The crack of the gunshot pierced the stillness, and the car lurched slightly as the tire deflated, succumbing to the puncture with a hiss.

"You got him," Gina exclaimed.

I tossed the gun into the trunk and then quickly slammed the lid shut. Without hesitation, I dove back into the car, our hearts racing as we tore down the highway.

As we drew closer, the glow of our headlights sliced through the darkness and illuminated the driver standing beside the back tire, peering down at the asphalt.

"Wouldn't it serve him right if we just sped by?" Gina huffed.

"It would sort of defeat the purpose of shooting out his tire," I reminded her.

Gina pulled over to the side of the road behind his car so we could use the headlights to illuminate the surroundings.

"Ready?" I asked as the car came to a complete stop.

"Let's do this," she replied.

As we stepped out into the cool night air, we headed towards the man. His oversized, sagging jeans hung precariously low, revealing a vivid red pair of boxers. Around his neck, a thick gold chain glimmered under the beam of the headlights. His head was shaved, and on the side was a tattoo of two crossed guns with a skull looming above them. He had the appearance of a teenage street thug.

As we approached, I noticed the tension in his shoulders, a flicker of wariness crossing his expression. He raised a hand to his forehead, shielding his eyes as he squinted into the brightness. As he recognized us, a wave of relief washed over him. He was probably happy we weren't law enforcement.

"Do you need some help?" I asked.

"Nah, it's just a flat," he replied. He hit a button on his key fab, which emitted a beep as the trunk popped open.

We ambled around to the back of the car, and he turned his back on us as he reached inside. Clearly, he didn't see us as a threat, but Gina and I exchanged glances, our minds racing to figure out our next move.

"We'll hang out in case you need any help," Gina said.

"Whatever," came his response as he removed the cooler and set it down at his feet. He delved back into the trunk.

Gina pointed at herself and then the cooler.

I nodded.

The thug hoisted out a spare tire, leaning it against the bumper, before retrieving the jack.

"Let me help," I offered, stepping closer to him with a determined smile. "I'm excellent at changing tires," I added, stopping strategically at the back corner of the vehicle, subtly obscuring the cooler from his view.

"Pfff," he scoffed, his disbelief evident as he shot me a sideways glance. It was as if he found the idea of me being capable utterly ludicrous.

I ignored the insult. "I used to watch my father change tires, and I can tell you the exact order to remove the lug nuts."

As he began to lift the car, I rambled on, trying to

distract him.

Gina strolled casually towards the cooler. She swiftly lifted the lid, peering inside with curiosity and determination. After a moment of hesitation, she let the lid drop, but unfortunately, it produced a loud swoosh as it closed.

He jumped to his feet. "What's going on? You two hussies trying to rob me?" He pulled out a switchblade, pointing it at me.

Instinctively, I took two steps back and pulled my gun. "Drop the knife if you want to see daybreak."

He leered at me but complied, his knife banging against the asphalt.

Gina retreated to her car, returning shortly with a zip tie, and quickly secured his hands behind his back.

At that moment, Krista's SUV drove past and pulled over in front of his car. With a flourish, she flung open the door and stormed out.

"How dare you," she exclaimed, striding towards the teen. "How could you leave a beautiful young woman stranded at the side of the road?"

He cast a deliberate gaze over her. "You ain't that young."

Krista looked taken aback. "Shoot him. Shoot him now," she said.

I shook my head. "Tell us about the cooler."

"I ain't telling you shit."

Gina glanced at me knowingly. We needed to interrogate the twerp, but time was slipping away. The longer we stood on the roadside, the higher the risk of being spotted.

"Now what," Krista asked.

"Now you go home," I replied firmly.

Krista pouted. "Why?"

"You can't be involved in what happens next. I'll call you later."

"Fine," she huffed, turning on her heel. "And you," she added, pointing an accusatory finger at the thug, "you better hope I don't run into you at the grocery store." With that, she stormed back to her car.

The thug raised an eyebrow, clearly unsure of how to respond to her.

I kept my gun pointed at the thug while Gina grabbed his shoulder and dragged him toward the Mustang.

He shook her hand off. "I ain't going nowhere with you ho's."

"You don't have a choice," I informed him. "But I don't want to hear your mouth the whole trip."

"We can't put him in the trunk," Gina said.

That was the understatement of the year. If we put him in there, he would easily find something to kill us with when we reopened the trunk.

"I know," Gina said, sprinting back to the car's trunk. Moments later, she emerged, gripping a roll of duct tape.

I arched an eyebrow as she swiftly tore off a strip and, in one practiced motion, pressed it firmly over the thug's mouth after he tried to dodge her efforts.

We maneuvered the teen into the back seat, and then we stowed the heavy cooler in the trunk

"Sit quietly," I told him as I slid into the car. "Or I'll shoot you in the leg."

I turned towards Gina. "Where can we go?"

"I know a place." She put the car in drive, and we took off.

Chapter 18

We pulled into the parking lot of a run-down motel on the outskirts of town. The once bright white siding was faded to a dull beige. A flickering neon red sign announced the establishment, but with two letters burned out, it now read 'Moe' instead of Motel. There was a rusted overflowing dumpster at the corner of the building with a small mountain of trash bags beside it.

"Nice place," I remarked dryly.

Gina parked next to the office, and I quickly climbed out. The doorknob felt as if it might snap off entirely as I twisted it open. Inside, a faint buzzing sound emanated from a bug zapper hanging in the corner, its light casting a sickly glow across the otherwise dim room.

The office appeared deserted, though a rhythmic snoring echoed from somewhere in the back. No bell was on the desk, so I rapped my knuckles against its sticky surface, a mysterious residue sticking to my hand. God only knew what it was. I would have to sanitize my hand with alcohol when I left this place. The snoring abruptly ceased, but no one emerged from the back room.

After a moment, I called out, "Hello."

"Hold your horses," came a gruff voice with a thick drawl that drifted out from behind.

I heard the unmistakable sound of hinges creaking as the foot of a recliner was lowered.

A man stepped through the doorway, his long

gray and black peppered hair falling well below his shoulders, matched by a beard that was just as unruly, almost obscuring the skin of his face. He wore a green shirt with so many stains I wondered if it had ever seen the inside of a washing machine. He looked me up and down, appraising my appearance.

"You sure you're at the right place?" he asked.

"I need to rent a room for an hour." I replied.

"Ah, so you're one of those. Fifty bucks."

"For an hour?" I raised an eyebrow. I expected it would be barely more than five dollars in a place like this.

"For the night," he replied, glancing around the dim lobby. "This may not be the Hilton, but we are not... that type of motel."

With a resigned sigh, I pulled the cash from my pocket and slapped it on the counter, making sure not to touch it again.

He stepped away from the counter, striding toward an ancient-looking boxed screen computer in the corner.

"Name?" he asked, fingers posed above the keys.

"Cinderella," I replied.

The corner of his lip hitched up. "Figured." He typed on the computer, then slid a key on a worn keychain, displaying a room number to me. "Whatever you're doing just keep the noise down. Don't want no complaints from your neighbors."

I found it hard to believe anyone else was staying in this classy establishment. "No problem," I assured him, taking the key and stepping outside into the warm evening air.

Gina quickly parked in front of our designated room, her eyes darting around to ensure we were alone. We swiftly ushered the thug into the room.

Inside, the hotel room featured a bed positioned at the center of the space and a wooden desk in one corner. The walls were covered in faded yellow floral wallpaper, with corners that sagged and peeled, revealing patches of dull white beneath. Heavy, yellow curtains framed a window that offered little light, the fabric hanging limply as if weighed down by years of neglect. At least the bedspread was crisp and white.

Gina yanked the wooden chair away from the desk and positioned our captor onto it. I grasped my pocketknife and sliced through the sturdy zip tie that bound his hands. Gina duct taped his wrist to the arms of the chair. With more joy than it required, Gina tore the duct tape from his mouth.

"What's your name, or do I refer to you as dead meat?" I asked.

He fought against the restraints for a brief moment. Tilting his face downward, he let the shadows mask his expression, but his cold, penetrating eyes flicked upward to meet mine.

"Call me Wraith," he said with a mix of confidence and defiance.

I figured this was his gang face that was supposed to scare us. Unfortunately for him, I didn't find him intimidating at all. The most evil men in the world didn't put on a facade and dress to get noticed. They avoided head tattoos and refrained from wearing body jewelry. Their hairstyles reflected the practicality of wealthy men, and they dressed in stylish designer clothes. They blended seamlessly into their surroundings, presenting an image of ordinary life so that you never suspected who they were until they were ready to strike.

"I've got this," Gina declared.

"You sure?"

She nodded firmly.

I flopped down onto the bed, the worn mattress groaning under my weight, sinking so deeply that it felt like I was lying directly on the floor. I propped my head against the ornate headrest. Gina sat at the edge of the bed, positioning herself in front of Wraith.

"So, Wraith," she began, her tone commanding, "this will go so much easier if you tell us everything you know about the cooler in your trunk. Whose is it, and where are you taking it?"

He glared at Gina but didn't say a word. Earlier, Gina shared with me that inside the cooler was a leg bone and what she believed to be a hip bone. I shifted to the edge of the bed and drummed my fingernails restlessly against the bedside stand. Patience had never been my strong suit.

Gina riffled through her purse, sitting on the bed beside her, and removed her gun.

"Hf," Wraith said with a sneer, "You can't shoot me. Someone will hear the gunshot." He sounded confident, calling her bluff.

She reached into her purse once more. After a moment, she withdrew a silencer and attached it to the end of the barrel, the click echoing in the stillness. She lowered her hand, pointing the gun at the floor.

"Tell us what we want to know so I don't have to shoot you."

"I don't have to tell you nothin," Wraith replied.

My little bit of patience had come to an end. I swiftly stood up and, at the same time, removed the chrome metal lamp from the nightstand, ripping the cord out of the wall. I strolled over to Wraith and, in one fluid motion, slammed the lamp into the side of his head. The lightbulb exploded on impact, and the chair toppled with him still in it.

Gina tapped her foot on the floor. She turned to me. "How do you feel?"

I rolled my shoulders, shaking off the lingering tension. "Better." Dropping the lamp onto the floor, I pulled the chair back up. There was now a bruise forming where the lamp met his skull and a cut that was slowly oozing blood.

"You better not have messed up my tat," he proclaimed angrily.

Unbelievable. Two unknown women kidnapped him, taped him to a chair, and threatened to shoot him, and he was only worried about a tattoo. His eyes darted between us. "You aren't going to do shit to me."

"Oh honey," Gina said. "You are delusional." She pointed the barrel of the gun at his hand. "Now tell us who gave you the cooler, or I'll blow off your pinky."

He said nothing and just continued to glare at us. I leaned over and whispered in Gina's ear.

She shrugged. "Works for me." She repositioned the gun, aiming between his legs.

His eyes widened, and he pushed himself back against the chair. "What are you doing?"

"If you don't tell us, I'll permanently change your gender," Gina said.

He tried to look confident, but glistening beads of sweat began to form on his forehead. I stifled a smile, aware of the absurdity of the situation. A man can adapt to life without a finger, but I had yet to encounter a man willing to forfeit his most treasured piece of masculinity.

"Fine," he huffed. "I don't know who sends the cooler."

"How do you not know?" I asked.

"I get a call to pick up the goods. I knock on the garage door when I arrive at the funeral home. The cooler slides out, I pick it up, and leave without seeing the person behind the door."

"How often do you make these pickups?" Gina chimed in.

"It varies," he replied. "Sometimes I'm there a couple of times a week, and others, I could go longer without a call."

"And where are you taking it?" I asked.

"To a place in D.C.," he replied casually.

"Could you be a little more specific?" Gina asked.

"I don't know who it goes to," he continued. "I deliver it to a building with a key stashed in a flowerpot next to the door. I unlock it and push the cooler inside, then walk away."

"You've never stepped inside to take a look around?" Gina inquired.

He shook his head.

Frustration welled up inside me, and I threw my arms up in exasperation. "What do you see when you crack open the door?"

"Looks like a waiting room," he said.

I began to pace the room. "So, you have no inkling of who's involved. Can you at least tell me what they're doing with the bones?"

"What?" Wraith asked, a flicker of genuine confusion crossing his face.

I halted in the middle of the room. "You have no idea what's in the cooler?"

Once more, he shook his head.

"So, let me get this straight," Gina challenged, her eyes narrowing in skepticism. "You could have been transporting drugs or laundered money, and you had no idea? You didn't care?"

"I get paid a lot of money not to pry inside those cases. I'm just the transporter," he replied.

"Who do you think you are," Gina scoffed. "Jason Statham?"

I stepped closer. "Listen to me," I said, my voice steady as I placed my hands firmly on the tops of his arms, leaning in until our faces were nearly inches apart. "As a transporter, if you are caught, you are just as responsible as the mastermind behind the crime." I watched the realization dawn in his eyes, a flicker of panic breaking through his facade. "You've been moving human remains. Think about it. If someone was murdered each time you transported a cooler, you would be charged as an accessory to those crimes. The consequences could land you in prison for a very long time."

As I fixed a steely glare on him, I watched his tough-guy facade begin to crumble under the weight of my words. For the first time, his expression morphed into one of genuine fear.

"I... don't want that kind of trouble! I'll tell you everything I know," he stammered, his voice cracking as desperation seeped into his tone. He quickly divulged the phone number for the caller responsible for pickups, followed by the address of the drop-off location. As he spoke, I noticed his gaze darting around the room anxiously, like a cornered mouse afraid the authorities might burst through the door at any moment.

I sighed and sat on the bed next to Gina. "Look," I said, my tone softening slightly. "We're going to take you back to your car. Fix your flat and head out of town. Call the number, tell him you were robbed, and the cooler was stolen, then lose that number. Forget you were ever involved in this mess. Trust me, the money isn't worth the risk."

He nodded.

"And forget about us," Gina said, her tone cold. "If you show up in my town again, I'll have no choice but to turn you into the cops."

His head bobbed up and down in quick, nervous motions, resembling a bobblehead doll swaying in agreement. "I don't want to go to jail," he admitted, his voice tinged with desperation.

Fifteen minutes later, we returned him to his car. I had never seen someone look so relieved to be stranded at the side of the road.

No sooner had we pulled away than my phone

rang. I quickly hit the speaker button, and Dominic's voice burst forth, laced with urgency.

"You aren't going to believe this," he said, and I could hear the excitement crackling in the air between us.

Chapter 19

"T.J. Rotz doesn't exist," Dominic declared.

"Come again?" I asked, caught off guard by the revelation.

"When I dug deeper into his background, I came up empty. It's as if he didn't exist until two years ago, as if he just materialized out of thin air," he continued.

"What does that mean?" Gina asked.

"It means he used to be someone else," I replied.

"Exactly," Dominic affirmed." His cover's so airtight that I had to hack into the CIA's database to find anything."

"Why would you do that?" I asked. All sorts of repercussions ran through my head, including some spooks showing up at his house in the middle of the night.

"Because they have the best facial recognition technology," he explained. "Don't worry. I was only there for a moment. I routed my access through multiple countries, so they won't be able to track me. I ran T.J.'s driver's license photo through the system and got a match for one Tyler Jenkins."

"Do you have any details about him?" I pressed.

"Boy, do I," Dominic replied. "Tyler has a troubled history with multiple arrests for burglary. Currently, there's an outstanding warrant for his arrest in Illinois, where authorities want him for questioning in connection with a homicide."

"Sounds like he could be our guy," I said.

"But he wasn't always working when someone died," Gina pointed out.

I took a moment to mull over her words, my mind racing through the possibilities. Then, suddenly, a realization struck me. "He left the door unlocked."

"Huh?" Gina said.

"Remember Shirley's complaint about him? She mentioned how he frequently forgot to secure the employee entrance. But what if it wasn't a simple mistake? What if he deliberately left it unlocked, allowing himself access whenever he pleased?"

"Then, when someone started searching for a suspect, they wouldn't even consider him. He had an alibi; he wasn't working every time someone met an untimely end," Dominic said.

"That's pretty smart," Gina conceded.

"Not smart enough," I replied. "Wonder where Tyler is now?"

"The Meadow Springs work schedule indicated that he was on the night shift, so he should be at work," Dominic said.

"Let's head over," Gina suggested.

"Dominic, I need you to find out everything you can about a phone number and address," I instructed, rattling off the digits that Wraith had given us.

"Got it," he replied before hanging up.

As we drove back towards town, a sudden thought struck me. "Let's make a detour to the funeral home first."

"Why would we do that?" Gina asked.

"It's clear Tyler's not working alone. Someone was at the funeral home and must have pushed that cooler out. They could still be inside."

Gina guided the car to a halt alongside the funeral home, its unsettling stillness casting an eerie cloud over the street.

"I'll go in. You wait here in case anyone shows up."

"It could be dangerous," Gina cautioned, her brow furrowing with concern.

"I doubt it. Whoever was in there is probably long gone by now. Besides, I can handle one person," I reassured her.

With stealth, I slipped into the shadows until I reached the side door of the building. I let myself in as I had before. As I ventured down the hall, my senses heightened. The door leading to the morgue loomed before me, wide open.

Voices echoed from the other side of the corridor. I instinctively drew my gun, its weight reassuring as I moved silently, my footsteps muted against the concrete floor. With each step, I focused on the distant voices.

The unmistakable tone of Rocco reverberated through the air. I wasn't surprised that he was involved.

"Get out of my morgue," he demanded, his voice a thunderclap that resonated through the cold, sterile space.

A second voice drifted out in response. "Calm down, Frankenstein. I'll be leaving soon enough."

"You're the one who keeps breaking in, aren't you?" Rocco asked.

I cautiously peeked around the corner and saw Tyler standing just a few steps from the heavy crematory door. He was holding a gun and had it pointed at Rocco's head. Rocco's hands were raised in the air.

"You picked a bad time to come to work. I just need to figure out what to do with you," Tyler said.

I quickly rounded the corner, pointing my gun at Tyler, "Drop your weapon," I yelled.

Tyler glanced in my direction, but his gun didn't move.

"Uh, Sydney. Why am I not surprised you're here? Drop your gun, or I'll shoot him."

"Go ahead," I bluffed as I moved further into the room, stopping in front of the freezer. "He means nothing to me. The more important question is whether his life is worth sacrificing your own."

Tyler's face fell, and I could tell he was unsure of his next move. Then, a sly smile creased his lips as I felt a gun press up against the back of my head.

"I think you need to drop your gun," A voice behind me stated.

I wondered why the bad guy always had an accomplice lurking in the shadows. My gun clanged against the floor as I raised my hands. Chloe moved up beside me with her gun trained on my head.

"I knew you were going to be trouble," she said. She cast a quick glance at Tyler, her eyes widening in shock, "Rocco, what are you doing here?"

"I was supposed to cremate Pearl before her funeral this morning." Rocco paused, a flicker of realization washing over his face. "Now I know who has been tampering with the bodies."

Chloe bit her bottom lip. "I wish you'd have stayed away," she murmured, her gaze shifting anxiously to Tyler. "Now, what do we do?"

Just then, the shrill tone of a ringing phone cut through the tense atmosphere like a knife. Tyler fished into his pocket with a swift motion to extract his phone.

"Hello," he greeted. I could make out a muffled response from the other end of the line. "You're never going to guess who's here," he added, shooting a glance my way. "Good guess." A moment of silence hung in the air, while Tyler listened to the voice on the other end. "You're the boss," Tyler concluded, a wry grin spreading across his face as he finally hung up the phone.

"Sorry, Sydney. It has been decided that you're

going to die tonight," he said with a hint of laughter in his eye.

Rocco took a step towards Tyler, but he caught the movement out of the corner of his eye and trained his attention back on Rocco.

"Don't even think of moving again," Tyler said.

The tension in the room was palpable.

"I have insulin," Chloe said, pulling a syringe from her purse. "It's enough to kill her in less than five minutes. After she's dead, we can cremate her."

I couldn't shake the unsettling thought of how many lives had been extinguished within the walls of that apartment building, potentially due to insulin overdoses. As I stood there, the gravity of my decision to go off alone weighed heavily on my mind; it was becoming painfully clear that I should have allowed Gina to come along for backup. I questioned whether Gina knew what was going on inside the morgue. What if she decided to check on me too late?

If I tried to lunge for Chloe's gun, she would just stab me with the needle. If I lunged for the syringe, she would shoot me. My only chance was to buy some time.

"One thing before you kill me. Can you tell me why you're stealing bones?"

Tyler's eyebrows arched up. "You don't know why. That's priceless. This is not a novel or a movie where I'm going to divulge everything to you. I guess you are going to die being left in suspense."

"Are you ready for me to stick her?" Chloe asked, a little too eagerly for my taste.

"Not quite yet. I haven't decided if I want to watch her slowly die," Tyler said, turning his gun towards me. "Or have the satisfaction of shooting her myself."

Without warning, a deafening explosion echoed through the room with such intensity that the walls trembled. This provided the distraction I needed. In an instant, I seized Chloe's wrist, rotating it around, and jabbed the needle into her thigh, pushing the plunger down.

She screamed, "I'm going to die!"

Tyler leveled his gun at me, but Rocco leapt forward, grabbing it. A shot rang out but hit the ceiling as they wrestled for the weapon. I yanked open a freezer drawer and slammed Chloe in the face with it while reaching for her gun. She covered her nose with her free hand but kept a tight grip on the pistol. I had no time to try to strip her of the gun. Using both my hands, I lifted the gun and used her finger to pull the trigger, shooting Tyler in the forehead. His eyes glazed over, and he dropped to the floor. I rammed my elbow into Chloe's throat. She let go of the gun and grabbed her throat, attempting to breathe. I pulled back and punched her in the face, knocking her out. Her head struck the floor with a dull thud.

"You okay?" I asked Rocco.

He nodded right before Gina jumped out of the corridor with her gun drawn, yelling, "Nobody moves."

Rocco's hands shot back up in the air.

"Don't worry," I said with a reassuring smile. "She's with me."

* * * *

We exited through the garage door, stepping into the cool night air that felt crisp against our skin. Just outside lay a car that was on fire. The fire crackled and popped like a distant thunderstorm, plumes of thick black smoke spiraling into the night sky, camouflaged by the darkness.

I turned to Gina. "You blew up a car?"

Gina shrugged nonchalantly, her gaze fixed on the fiery wreck. "It was Tyler's. Figured he deserved it."

"How did you know it was his?" I asked.

"Vanity plates," she replied with a sly grin. "It said 'TJ's Ride.'"

Before long, the wail of sirens pierced the air as the fire trucks arrived. We stood off to the side in the grass, watching as the firefighters worked to extinguish the flames.

Shortly after their arrival, an unmarked black patrol car slid to a halt at the curb. Sean and Blake emerged from the vehicle, their expressions betraying irritation as they strode across the yard, clearly not thrilled to see us.

"Why am I not surprised to find you here?" Blake remarked dryly, his eyes narrowing slightly.

In response, Gina and I exchanged glances and, without uttering a word, pointed deliberately toward the entrance of the morgue.

Blake hesitated momentarily, his gaze shifting to Rocco, who gave a subtle nod. With a resigned sigh, Blake ambled over to peek inside the structure.

"I'm out twenty bucks," Sean declared. "When the call came in about a car fire at the morgue, I bet Blake you two weren't involved. I should have played the odds."

Blake yelled back for Sean, and he sprinted inside the morgue.

"We're going to be here awhile," Gina said, her tone casual as she flopped down onto the grass. She rummaged through her purse and finally pulled out a pack of Oreo cookies.

"Do you want one?" she inquired.

"Are they double stuffed?" I replied.

"Of course."

Rocco and I sat down beside Gina on the hard ground. We savored the cookies as we watched an ambulance pull into the lot. Two paramedics leaped out and hurriedly pushed a stretcher inside. A short time later, they reemerged, wheeling out Chloe on the stretcher; an oxygen mask clung to her face.

"Guess she's still alive," Gina remarked.

"I probably should have killed her. It would make the questioning easier," I said.

Gina smiled, a glint of mischief dancing in her eyes. "Live and learn."

"What prompted the explosion?" I asked.

She leaned back, recalling the sequence of events. "You had barely slipped into the building when Chloe arrived. After she disappeared inside, I waited a few minutes before I followed. A lot of yelling was coming from the morgue, and I heard Tyler's voice. It struck me that you might need a diversion. And honestly, what better distraction is there than a good old-fashioned explosion?"

Relief washed over me as I replied, "I'm glad you did."

"Me too," Rocco said.

The flames on the engulfed car were now extinguished, leaving behind a charred, twisted metal husk that exhaled faint puffs of smoke. The firefighters had turned off their hoses and began packing up their equipment.

Blake stormed over. "What the hell happened here?"

Gina threw her hands up in an innocent gesture. "I was outside the whole time."

"Thanks," I said. "Gina and I were driving by and noticed the side door to the funeral home was ajar. I decided to get out and close it."

Blake raised an eyebrow. "You just happened to be driving by in the middle of the night?" he questioned, skepticism coloring his tone.

"We couldn't sleep after what happened at the

bar," I answered, glancing sideways at Gina, who nodded.

"And I was dying for some ice cream," Gina chimed in. "Oops, pun not intended." She laughed. "Anyway, there was no ice cream at the house, so I figured I could swing by the all-night convenience store on Glen Street."

Blake looked at us as if he didn't believe a word we had said. "Continue."

I took a breath and plunged back into the story, recounting everything from the voices in the morgue to the shocking moment when the car erupted into flames outside.

"When you heard people inside, why didn't you call the police?" Blake demanded.

"I heard Rocco's voice and just assumed he was working late," I replied. "I was just going to let him know the door was open. I didn't realize the gravity of the situation until it was too late."

Blake pinched the bridge of his nose, a telltale sign of his frustration with me. I noticed he did that a lot, and I couldn't help but wonder if anyone else in his life irritated him enough to elicit such a reaction.

"So, after the explosion, you plunged the syringe into Chloe?" Blake asked. "The very one she intended to use on you?"

I nodded.

"Then who shot Tyler?" Blake pressed.

Before I could muster a plausible explanation, Rocco spoke up. "Chloe shot him. She was so flustered when the needle jabbed into her leg that she accidentally pulled the trigger. I honestly don't think she meant to hit him."

Blake glanced at us, shaking his head in exasperation. "You two are lucky to be alive," he said, addressing both Rocco and me.

Turning to Gina, he demanded, "What happened

to the car?"

Gina looked back at him with wide eyes, feigning innocence. "How should I know?" she replied

Blake raised his arms in frustration. "You said you were outside."

Gina gestured towards her car, which was parked along the curb beside the building. "I was over there in the car. When I heard the explosion, I dashed inside to make sure Sydney was okay."

"This isn't the end. There's someone else involved," I added.

"Why do you think that?" Blake questioned.

"While Tyler had his gun aimed at us, he answered his phone. He spoke to the caller like he was in charge, referring to him as 'the boss.'"

Blake's expression darkened as he absorbed that information.

A police car pulled into the driveway, the blue and red lights cutting through the evening dusk. Blake strode over to speak with the officer.

"Thanks for covering for me," I said to Rocco.

If the police learned about Tyler's death at my hands, it would inevitably ignite an investigation. My superior would surely be furious, and I risked losing my cover.

Rocco gave me a crooked smile. "Thanks for saving my life. I owe you one. And call me Lurch. My friends do," he said in his deep voice.

With a slight awkwardness, he leaned to the side, struggled to push himself up, and then ambled away, his gait stiff and uncertain.

I knew it.

Gina stifled a yawn, weariness etched on her face. "I'm beat," she murmured, her shoulders drooping as we prepared to leave the scene.

"Hold on," Sean interjected, his tone slicing

through the air. Blake caught his cue, and together they approached us.

"I'm not done with you two yet," Sean said, his voice brimming with irritation. "I can't even begin to explain how irresponsible your actions were tonight." He took a breath, visibly trying to steady himself. "I'm just relieved you didn't drag Krista into this mess."

As he spoke, I saw Dominic dashing down the driveway, his figure a blur of frantic movement. A uniformed officer stopped him.

"Are you even listening to me?" Sean's voice rose.

I pointed toward Dominic. "I think you should let him pass."

Blake and Sean turned to see Dominic bouncing from one foot to the other, wildly waving the green notebook above his head like a trophy.

"I've got it!" Dominic shouted.

Sean looked at Blake who merely shook his head.

"Let him by," Blake bellowed toward the officer, frustration evident in his tone. "This can't possibly get any weirder."

He was wrong.

Chapter 20

"I know what's going on," Dominic pronounced proudly as he hurried over to us.

"Well?" Blake demanded, his impatience palpable as he shifted his weight, crossing his arms.

"They were selling the bones," Dominic revealed.

I glanced at Gina. "We figured that out, but why?"

Dominic produced a wide smile. "For the stem cells," he explained.

Gina's brow knotted into an inquisitive frown. "What?"

"Stem cells," Dominic elaborated. "They're the vital blood cells found in bone marrow. Right now, stem cells are at the cutting edge of medical research. Scientists are harnessing them to treat cancer and other devastating diseases."

He paused, fishing something from his pocket. "The phone number you gave me was linked to a burner phone, but I managed to uncover this."

He handed me a piece of computer paper, but before my eyes could scan the information, Blake snatched it from my grasp with a quick motion. I leaned in, peering over his shoulder, and saw a man clad in a stark white lab coat.

"That's Dr. Mark Crowwell," Dominic said. "He's the premier doctor in stem cell research." He pointed at the address on the paper. "He also owns the building you mentioned. That's where he sees his patients."

"So, they're stealing bones and selling them to this doctor?" Blake asked.

Dominic nodded.

"But why kill people for it?" Gina asked.

"For the money," Dominic replied, his tone matter-of-fact.

Sean leaned forward, intrigued yet skeptical. "How much can a bone be worth?" he asked.

"A lot," Dominic replied. "When a person donates bone marrow, they harvest less than ten percent of the stem cells, and that is worth ten thousand dollars."

Sean's eyes widened, and he whistled softly.

"Holy crap," Gina exclaimed. "So, each bone could be worth around a hundred grand?"

"Pretty much," Dominic confirmed.

"Wait... Hold on," Blake interrupted. "Who has been killed?"

Gina and I exchanged glances, a silent understanding passing between us before we took turns revealing the details of our investigation into the troubling deaths at the nursing home. We relayed how the CEO, Thomas, had initially hired us to uncover the truth behind these suspicious incidents, but had abruptly terminated our services earlier today.

Blake ran his hand down his face in a weary gesture, frustration evident in his eyes, while Sean stood frozen, his mouth slightly agape in shock. "How will we ever know how many bodies are involved?" Sean finally asked. "This is so much worse than we thought."

"Oh, it gets better, "Dominic piped up excitedly, bouncing on his heels like a child with a secret. "I decoded Charlie's notebook."

Blake shot me a burning glare, frustration etched

across his face. "I don't remember you mentioning a notebook."

I gave him an apologetic smile.

Dominic's eyes flickered nervously between us as if trying to gauge the temperature of the escalating confrontation. "We were planning to hand it over just as soon as I figured out what the coded messages meant," he interjected, attempting to steer the conversation back on track.

"I'm sure," Blake replied, his tone dripping with doubt.

Dominic began to flip through the worn pages of the notebook in question. "I don't know why, but Charlie kept a record of every person he took bones from. He even noted which bone it was," he explained.

"That's sort of creepy," Gina said.

I leaned in, eager to uncover more. "Did Charlie happen to mention the names of any of his accomplices?" I asked.

Dominic nodded. "Close to the end, I think Charlie wanted out. He not only wrote the names of his three accomplices but also compiled a list of victims they killed. I guess he thought this notebook would serve as insurance to keep him alive. I made a list of both."

He pulled out a neatly typed set of pages stapled together and handed it to Blake. Blake turned his back on me, focusing intently on the page, only to frown deeply, the weight of the revelations sinking in and how far the dark path had led.

"This is quite a list of victims," Sean said, reading over Blakes shoulder.

"I want to see," Gina insisted as she crossed her arms.

"Police business," Blake replied tersely.

Aware of who else was involved, Dominic leaned closer as he divulged the name. Gina leaned in, straining to catch every syllable.

Blake pursed his lips, casting a disapproving glance at us.

I wasn't surprised when I heard the name.

"Are you going to arrest him?" Gina inquired, her eyes wide with anticipation.

Flipping over the first page of notes, Blake began skimming the second, his brow furrowing with concentration. "There's definitely enough information here to bring him in for questioning," he stated, his tone all business. "Sean, what do you think?"

Sean frowned. "Judge Daniels is out of town until tomorrow afternoon."

"So?" Dominic asked.

"We need a warrant," Blake stated.

"You have got to be kidding," I exclaimed, my frustration spilling over. "You know he's guilty."

"It doesn't matter," Sean replied. "We can knock on his door, but we can't forcibly enter the house without a warrant."

Blake continued, "He's smart enough to know that, so even if he is home, he won't answer the door."

"But by tomorrow afternoon, he'll be halfway to Mexico," I insisted.

"Or Canada," Gina said.

"There are laws we have to follow," Blake stated firmly.

I blew out a breath in frustration. As soon as he caught wind of the incident at the morgue, he'll hastily pack his bags and vanish.

Just then, a spark of inspiration flickered in Gina's eyes. "I have an idea," she declared, raising her pointer finger.

One word never sounded so scary.

* * * *

Upon entering the house, we slowly looked around. The spacious open floor plan made it easy to note that there was no life in the main living area.

"Let's head towards the hallway," I instructed, clutching Gina's phone, its screen glowing. We stood in the front yard as the early morning light of dawn unfurled across the sky. With a push, Gina maneuvered the joystick forward, and Marti's engine roared to life, a low buzzing resonating through the phone as it glided across the living room floor. It came to a halt at the far end of the hallway.

Gina navigated a different joystick, guiding the camera lens to scan our surroundings. On either side of the hallway, two doorways beckoned, two on the right left ajar, while two doors stood firmly closed on the left.

"He's probably hiding in one of those rooms," I suggested, pointing at the closed doors on the left side of the screen.

Gina guided Marti toward the first door. With a few deft clicks, she activated the mechanism. Through the phone screen, I watched Marti's metallic claw arm extended, fingers splayed as it latched onto the doorknob, twisting it with a precise, almost mechanical grace. The door swung open effortlessly to reveal a bathroom.

Everything shimmered in a dull, powdery blue. The walls, tub, and even the toilet were this stagnant light blue hue.

"Yuck," Gina grimaced. "Looks like a throwback to the eighties in here."

The floral shower curtain, a garish spectacle with blue and yellow flowers, hung open, revealing an empty tub. With nowhere else to hide, Marti turned and motored down to the next door. His claw arm once more reached for the knob, gripping it firmly. Just as he began to turn it, we heard shuffling sounds from within.

"I know that's you, Sydney. If you come through that door, I'll blow your head off."

I glanced at Gina, who merely smiled, her eyes glinting with determination. She deftly manipulated the controller, guiding Marti as he turned the doorknob with steady precision. With a resounding click, the door unlocked.

A gunshot shattered the silence. My eyes darted to the camera feed, but there was no visible alteration to the door, leading me to conclude that the shooter had aimed higher than Marti's line of sight. Without hesitation, Gina pushed the joystick forward, and the door creaked open slowly as Marti moved along his designated path.

As Marti entered the room, the camera shifted its focus to Sheriff Earl, who loomed ominously in front of a wooden desk. It appeared to be a small, cluttered office. On the desk rested a closed suitcase, sitting next to a bright red gas can. Clearly, he had devised a plan to torch any evidence to cover his tracks before fleeing.

"You think your little toy can stop me," he said before firing two shots that echoed through the small room.

Since Marti's camera was still focused on the sheriff, I assumed he had missed his target.

"You'd think being sheriff, he'd be a better shot," I said.

Gina looked furious. "He shot at my robot!" she exclaimed. "How dare he."

Gina focused intently on her controller, her fingers dancing over the buttons with practiced precision. Meanwhile, Marti's arm extended toward the hook that jutted out from his front. Earl, seemingly oblivious until now, watched in shock as his gaze followed the claw's movement toward the hook, his eyes widening in astonishment at the unexpected sight.

I could hear the soft, metallic scrape as Marti's claw gripped the object hanging from the hook, making a distinct click as it pulled away. Through the camera, I saw the claw gripping a grenade. The pin was missing, assumably left dangling behind on the hook.

Earl narrowed his eyes. "You wouldn't dare," he challenged.

I pressed the unmute button on the phone. "Why should you be granted another chance, considering all the lives lost, including the two who mysteriously died in your jail cells?" I queried, my voice steady and laced with accusation.

For a moment, he seemed to waiver the confidence in his sneer faltering. "You have no proof I was involved," he shot back.

"I have a feeling that if we dig enough in the hole in my backyard, we might unearth the bullet that ended Charlie's life," Gina proposed. "What are the odds it will match your gun?"

The sheriff's smile faded as he took another shot at the robot.

"That's it," Gina declared suddenly. With a swift motion, she pressed the bright red button on the center of the controller, and Marti's metallic claw sprung open. The grenade clanged against the hardwood floor. Earls' expression shifted to sheer shock as he raced past Marti.

Gina gave me a high five.

We expected him to run out the back door, so we were surprised when he came barreling out the front door of the house instead. Spotting us on the front lawn, his features twisted into a furious scowl. He started to raise his arm with the gun, but a loud bang rang out.

Earl instinctively leaped off his porch. He landed hard on his stomach and covered his head with his hands. His gun slipped from his grasp, quietly landing in the soft grass in front of him. After a few seconds, he cautiously peered up. To his astonishment, he spotted us standing there, an air of nonchalance enveloping us as we smiled down at him.

Earl spotted his gun, but before he could reach for it, Blake and Sean ran around the corner of the house, guns drawn.

"Don't move," They both shouted in unison.

"I'm the sheriff around here," Earl bellowed as they shoved his hands behind his back, and Blake handcuffed him.

As Blake began to recite the familiar rights, Earl's voice cut through the air. "You can't arrest me. You illegally broke into my house without a warrant."

"I didn't break into your house," Blake countered. He turned to Sean. "Did you?"

"Nope," Sean replied, shaking his head with a casual indifference.

Blake turned towards us.

"We were standing near the sidewalk, minding our own business," I replied.

The sheriff shot me a venomous glare as Sean led him away toward the patrol car.

"There should be enough evidence for the D.A.'s office," Blake said, rubbing his chin. "It's a shame all the bones went to Washington. Having one of them would strengthen our case."

"The trunk of my car is unlocked," Gina said. "There might be a cooler in there that you'll want to check."

Blake's eyebrow shot up, and he made his way toward the car with measured strides. I leaned closer to Gina, lowering my voice. "I can't believe you left the trunk unlocked. What if someone had decided to rob us?"

She dismissed my concern with a casual wave of her hand. "Nobody wants human bones," she replied with a grin.

I raised an eyebrow at her.

"Well, normal people don't."

Blake's figure vanished behind the trunk lid, only to reappear moments later, casting a curious glance back at us. "You know what? I don't even want to know where you got these," he said.

"You can trace them back to a body currently at the morgue," I stated flatly.

He nodded, lifting the cooler from the trunk.

"We'll look into it," he said.

The sheriff glanced up in surprise as Blake maneuvered the cooler past the side of the patrol car.

"Guess Earl thought that was long gone," I remarked.

Gina flashed a triumphant smile. "We did good. Now, let's get Marti."

We climbed the stairs.

"By the way, what was that loud bang we heard earlier?" I asked.

"I'll show you."

Marti was still in the study, surrounded by a chaotic splatter of vibrant lime green paint that adorned the walls and floor. As Gina handed me the remote, a hint of amusement danced in my expression when I stepped into the room.

"You set off a paint grenade?"

Gina chuckled softly, glancing at the robot covered in the paint splatters. "Poor Marti. You're going to need a bath when we get home,"

She lifted the robot as we exited the house, leaving behind the vibrant chaos.

Chapter 21

Two days later, I found myself in the kitchen savoring a warm cup of coffee while relishing the silence. Wilber's owner had come to collect him yesterday, much to the chickens' chagrin. To ensure a restful night, I locked my bedroom door, effectively discouraging any feathered visitors, and as a result, I enjoyed the best night's sleep I'd experienced since arriving in town.

I was halfway through my steaming cup when a sudden beeping sound pierced the tranquility from the backyard.

"What's that noise? "Gina asked as she entered the kitchen.

"Let's take a look," I replied, unable to suppress a smile as I rose to my feet.

We stepped outside and spotted a truck maneuvering in reverse toward the gate at the far end of the fence. Just the day before, a construction crew had filled the gaping hole in the backyard, and there sat the chickens, their heads cocked as they eyed the approaching vehicle.

As the truck halted behind the gate, Gina could barely contain her excitement. She leaped up and down in a burst of uncontainable joy. "You bought a new chicken coop!" she exclaimed, dashing towards the gate and throwing it open.

The new chicken coop had wooden plank walls

adorned in a turquoise blue. A black metal slanted roof crowned the structure, while a small window framed in white trim offered a glimpse of the interior.

As the chickens clucked and shuffled about, they instinctively moved aside, allowing the coop to take the spot where the old shed had once stood. Elevated on four legs, the coop sat a foot above the ground, and a ramp resembling a gangplank led up to a small opening.

Gina rushed over, her eyes alight with excitement as she swung open the large side door and peered inside. "It's got nesting boxes for eggs and even a bar for them to perch on to sleep at night!" she exclaimed, her voice bubbling with delight.

I glanced down to find Lacey regarding me with her head cocked to the side.

"Make no mistake, I'm not being nice," I said firmly. "I simply don't want you sleeping in my room again."

She studied me for a moment before leaning over to affectionately nuzzle the soft feathers of her head against my leg. A smile crept onto my face as I watched her waddle off. She scampered up the gangplank, with Cagney trailing closely behind her.

* * * *

Gina wanted to decorate the area around the coop to make it look as nice as the new structure. I devoted the afternoon to helping her spread grass seed beneath the coop. Afterward, we planted colorful flowers around the sturdy legs of the coop. Cagney, perched at the top of the gangplank, kept a watchful eye on us.

After dinner, I went upstairs, eager to wash away the remnants of our labor. The warm water enveloped me in the shower, soothing my tired muscles and rinsing away the dirt from planting flowers. Just as I toweled off, an unexpected chill ran down my spine, a shiver that alerted me to the presence of someone else in the room.

"Hello?" I called out. There was no reply. I draped the towel around myself and cautiously opened the door to peer out. To my surprise, Krista sat on my bed, her back turned to me.

"You scared me," I said, feeling an unsettling tension in the air.

Krista remained silent, not acknowledging my presence. As I stepped closer, the sight of my bedspread came into focus, and a wave of dread washed over me.

Sitting on the bed before Krista was a Japanese ornamental jewelry box, its wooden surface polished to a soft sheen. The lid featured a delicate carving of a Japanese cherry tree. I recalled that Gina had gifted me this treasure one Christmas. The interior was lined with crimson silk. Though I didn't have much jewelry to place inside, I found it the perfect holder for my passport, military ID, and a few bills, making it my constant companion on countless journeys.

What made this box special was a cleverly concealed compartment that required an intricate series of maneuvers to unlock. Unfortunately, that same Christmas, Gina gave Krista a similar jewelry box, making her the only person privy to its secrets. As I looked at Krista, the hidden drawer lay open, revealing a shocking array of contents: two foreign passports, a German visa, and a substantial wad of cash in euros.

She held a small listening device in her grasp. I felt a weight of apprehension settle over me as I stood frozen, the words stuck in my throat. Krista didn't look up; her gaze remained fixed on the objects laid out before her. The silence between us felt palpable, stretching into an uncomfortable eternity as both of us grappled with the sudden reveal. Finally, she gently placed the bug atop the money pile and lifted the Italian passport.

"I was being nosey while I waited for you to get out of the shower," she remarked, her voice laced with betrayal. "You're not a nurse," she said, a statement of fact rather than a question.

"No."

She gestured at the passport in her hand. "That's your picture, but it carries a name that isn't yours." Her gaze finally locked onto mine, piercing and filled with confusion. "Are you some kind of spy?"

I shook my head. "No, I'm not a spy. I do serve in the army. I'm a Counterintelligence Agent."

Silence enveloped her as she absorbed my words, her expression shifting from suspicion to something darker. "Have you ever killed anyone?" she asked barely above a whisper.

"Yes," I replied, honesty spilling out at that moment. I decided I was done lying to her. She deserved to know the truth.

"So... you are a killer for the government?" she recoiled slightly.

"No," I replied gently as I sat on the bed next to her. "I could never be an assassin. The only times I've taken a life were in self-defense or to protect someone else."

"What do you do then?" she pressed.

With a heavy sigh, I explained, "I work with a team to track down bad guys."

"Like drug dealers?" she asked, her brow furrowing in concern.

"Yes," I nodded. "And arms traffickers, and terrorists... It's a dangerous world out there. I never told you because I wanted to shield you from worry. It was safer for you if you remained oblivious to the truth. Believe me, I wanted nothing more than to tell you the truth."

I reached for her hand, but she withdrew, pulling

away as if my touch burned. "Trust you?" she sobbed, her voice cracking under the weight of her emotions. "I don't even know you."

She leaped off the bed, her feet barely touching the floor, before she bolted out of the room. I scrambled after her, clutching my towel tightly with one hand. "Krista, wait!" I called out, my voice echoing through the hallway as she dashed down the stairs.

In the living room, Gina rose from the couch, her eyes wide with concern as Krista reached the front door. "Krista, are you okay?" she asked.

Krista paused, one hand resting on the doorknob, and I halted at the bottom of the stairs, bracing myself for what would come next. She slowly turned to face Gina, her expression a mix of confusion and hurt.

"Did you really have a desk job designing airplanes when you were in the military?" Krista inquired.

Gina nervously glanced at me before responding. "I was an international bomb expert," she finally confessed.

"I see," Kista whispered as a tear rolled down her cheek.

She stepped through the doorway, the door closing gently behind her with a near-silent finality. My shoulders slumped as a wave of despair washed over me.

Don't worry," Gina said softly, stepping closer to me, and she placed a comforting hand on my shoulder. "She just needs time to process it all. She'll come around."

"I hope so," I replied, my voice barely above a whisper, as I continued to stare at the closed door.

* * * *

That evening, I attempted to relax on the front

porch swing, hoping to soak in the tranquility of the evening. However, the anxiety swirling inside me after my encounter with Krista made it nearly impossible to find peace. With a sigh, I decided to go for a jog to clear my mind. I laced up my sneakers and set off at a moderate pace.

As I ran, I tried to banish Krista's face from my thoughts. But no matter how hard I pushed myself, I couldn't forget the look of betrayal in her eyes.

As I rounded the corner, heading back toward Gina's house, I finally surrendered to the pain and exhaustion and slowed to a stop. Catching my breath, I continued at a leisurely pace.

There was no activity on the street. The temperature had dropped, and the sun was starting to dip behind the mountains. When I was two houses down from Gina's, the whine of a poorly tuned engine broke the stillness. I turned to see Blake's rusted green truck chugging up the road, smoke trailing behind it like a ghost. He passed by without a glance and pulled in Gina's driveway. I arrived moments later to find him leaning against the trunk, waiting for me.

"Army," he greeted, a grin spreading across his face.

"Robocop," I replied.

His smile widened. "I assume you've been following the case as it's been unfolding on the news?"

I shook my head. "I don't watch the news. There are just too many grim stories crowding the airwaves." I responded, my thoughts as I reflected on the myriad of news stories I had caused through my covert operations.

He chuckled and crossed his arms. "Dr. Crowwell was arrested this morning. There's a video of them escorting him out of his office in handcuffs. The FBI is launching a thorough investigation, suspecting that our morgue isn't the only one involved in this scandal. They found ten times more bone marrow stuffed in his freezer than even the University had known about."

"Interesting," I replied, leaning back against the vehicle beside him. "And what about the home front?"

"Chloe's awake," he said. "She doesn't remember shooting Tyler, but she admits to her memory going blank right after being injected with the insulin. She does, however, have several bruises on her face and a broken nose." He arched an eyebrow. "You said that you only punched her in the throat to get her to drop the gun."

"Must have happened when she fell," I said with a cold expression that revealed nothing.

"She was lying on her back," he pointed out.

"She must have rolled over."

Blake flashed a grin, shaking his head. "Anyway, she's rolling on the Sheriff, hoping for a reduced sentence."

"Good," I replied, pushing off the car and heading toward the front door.

"I have to add," Blake continued, quickening his pace to catch up with me, "even though I appreciate the information you gathered for the case, I need you to stay out of police business for the rest of your vacation." His tone was serious.

I halted abruptly. "Really?"

As if that would happen.

"Promise me," he insisted.

"Ha! I'm living with Gina. You know I'll be dragged into whatever mess she gets herself into."

"I thought I would at least try," he replied, shaking his head in mock defeat as I ascended the staircase.

As I reached the top, my attention was drawn to a brown box in front of the door. Upon closer inspection, I noted that my name and Gina's address were typed on in, yet there was no return address to provide any clues.

"What's this?" I thought out loud.

"A box," Blake stated.

"No kidding, Sherlock, but who's it from?"

"You would know better than I would," he replied, turning away. "Always nice talking to you. See you around." He strolled back to his truck. I waited until he drove away before returning my attention to the box.

I picked it up, noticing that it wasn't heavy. Maybe my partner had sent me something. I placed the box on the table beside the rocking chair. I drew my knife with a steady hand, cutting the tape that sealed the flaps shut. I tucked my knife back into my pocket.

As I opened the flaps, the sudden sound of a whirring fan filled the air, startling me. Before I could comprehend what was happening, a burst of glitter exploded from the box, shooting up into the sky like a geyser. I instinctively shut my eyes and stumbled backward. When I finally reopened my eyes, I was astonished. A cascade of vibrant pink glitter soared into the air, catching the sunlight and shimmering like a thousand tiny stars as it floated back down to the earth. Once plain and dull, the porch was now covered in sparkling pink glitter, including me. I could feel the fine particles settling into my hair.

I HATE the color pink.

Just then, my phone buzzed insistently in my pocket. I fished it out, glancing down to find my arm completely draped in the shimmery pink dust. A sigh escaped my lips as I looked at my screen.

"Now we're even," the text stated.

My gaze shot upward to see Blake sitting in his truck across the street. A mischievous grin plastered across his face that seemed to stretch from ear to ear. With a wave, he pulled away and drove down the street

"What's going on?" I heard Gina's voice behind me.

As I turned to face her, her eyes widened in disbelief. "You're covered in glitter," she exclaimed, laughter bubbling up through her surprise. "And pink at that. How'd this happen?" She glanced down at the empty box that once contained the iridescent sparkles but was now silent.

"Blake," I replied.

"Well, I guess you two are even now," she chuckled.

But as the last remnants of pink glitter drifted down from the sky like delicate fairy dust, I shook my head firmly. "Oh, no," I said, the resolve in my tone unmistakable. "This is far from over."

Visit Misty on her website at **www.mistylynnbooks.com**

Or follow her on Facebook at **Misty Lynn-Books**

If you liked the book, take a moment to leave a review.